The Old Farts Allotment

Mick Reilly

Contents

Chapter 1

The Flying Slug

The sign outside the pub said it was called 'The Snug', a name which conjured up images of open fires, sleeping dogs and of old men playing dominoes while smoking pipes, but, there was never a pub a more aptly renamed than "The Flying Slug".

Inside it was quite a different picture. No cosy warm glow to be had in here. It was just a pub. It was a pub where men went without their wives, where adults went without kids. It was pub where people went after having eaten at home or having fallen off the last bus back home from their sojourns into wildly exotic places like Dolethorpe. It was a pub that, despite the occasional begrudged splash of emulsion, had managed to retain a 1950's dour ambience of "What's tha want? Food... food! This is a pub, we sell beer ere."

The cry, "Aye, and it's so strong 'e as to wata it down" would generally come from someone lurking within the firing zone of the blistered and faded dart board.

Challenged to get modern and worried about local competition the landlord hung, above the redundant fireplace, a huge flat screen TV which, to the pleasure of some and the annoyance of most, seemed to show continuous football matches and at which, for some strange reason, young men would stand obediently looking upwards in reverence whilst shouting guidance to blind referees and instructions to some players that they should go forth and procreate!

The only saving grace was that the television sound was turned off so the barmaid could listen to the jukebox, "songs from my era…. when singers could sing, 'Ar luv it' was her rebuke to anyone asking for more up to date thump, thump, thumping!

This single act of installing a plasma TV probably did more to send customers huffing and puffing up the hill to the "Cock Inn" than the promise of viewing the barmaid there, 'Luscious Lucy' in her Bingo Bra… Eyes down look in!

A lovely lass but her intelligence was never as big as her assets.

"Two pints of cider luv."
"Watud yu lark, sweet or dry?"
"As thee any o' that Dickens?"
"Dickens?" "I've not eard o" that!"
"Tha nus 'Dick-in-cider'!"…. Some nights it was worth the uphill struggle!

It was the ban on smoking in public places that caused the pub to be renamed. Prior to then smokers never ventured outside unless the gents toilet was full. Until then users, of the patch of grass laughingly called a beer garden, would remark on the number of slugs they could see. The landlord would explain that the spilt beer attracted them, though how the watered down beer sold there could be found desirable to any slugs intent on a drink induced suicide was anyone's guess besides…. what were they doing on the tarmac car park?

Forced to go outside and smoke, "this fresh air is mekin me coff wus." It wasn't long before the smokers saw the occasional slug flying over the fence from the allotments!

"Ay up gaffer, them ol'farts from 'llotments are chucking slugs ower thee fence"

"Nah, it'll be birds dropping them" commented 'Windy' Millar from the relative safety of the main entrance or in cases of conflict such as now, the emergency exit!

"Chuff off thee, thar's gorra 'llotment, thar's bound tu say it. We jus sin it appenin, 'sides… thar's a Suthern puff!"

"What are you smoking? Flying slugs, whatever next, "Snails on skate boards!" replied 'Windy' amazed at his own retort. "Must tell the missus about that one" he thought.

It was into this affray that Mick 'Gob on Legs' O'Rearden walked.

"'Ere's another un gaffer…. One o' them ol'farts slinging slugs ower thee fence!

"Ayup, oo yow callin n olfart?" asked O'Rearden. "One, I ain't old, well, mebbee I'm more mature than yow lot, an' two, I ain't a fart. Where I come from that term of endearment is reserved for Yorkshur men… yu know them smelly bags of shite that emanate from the arses of their 'Geordie' neighbours!

In any other pub in Yorkshire this would have been fighting talk but here in 'The Snug' it passed for banter. The landlord duly pulled a pint and with a steely eye asked "any truth in that then?"

"Cum on gaffer, yer asking the wrong bloke, ask the 'Lockie Sheriff' when 'e cums in, he's in charge not me."

Chapter 2

The Allotments

The Allotments, all 40 plots, were originally tenanted to coal miners who worked at Frighall Colliery. Back in 1947 the pit became part of the National Coal Board and, wishing to enamour themselves with the pit workers, the NCB released a parcel of land, on which they held mineral rights, for the purpose of recreational gardening…. recreational gardening…. Biggest misnomer ever made!

There wasn't a pit worker who didn't use his plot for personal commercial gain whether it was flogging eggs, knackered hens, breeding and slaughtering rabbits or gerrin shut of surplus tatties, onions, cabbages etc. and, occasionally, the odd bunch of sweet peas… but then, they were only from the girlie miners. Oh, yes, they were about then, but you only found out in the pit head baths when you dropped your soap!

Back in the forties they saw no reason not to call themselves 'Frighall Allotments and Garden Society' or 'FAGS' as it conjured up memories of them smoking 'Park Drive', 'Woodbines' or 'Capstan Full Strength' cigarettes. 'Fags' were what they all smoked, 'Coughing Nails', 'Cigs', 'Nub Ends', 'Roll Ups', 'Cancer Sticks' and in hard times… even tea leaves rolled up in baccy paper!

Had they realised that the kids of their 'London Swank' gaffers, who went to private school and who became slaves to the older boys, were to be known as 'FAGS 'or that eventually American homosexuals were also to become known as 'FAGS' they would have chosen a different name, but names stick but then, so does "Arl knock thee chuffin 'ead off if tha teks piss enymoor."

The allotments weren't big, when compared to those in towns and cities, but here in a rural Yorkshire village they occupied a sizable piece of land and best of all it was free, well almost!

Each miner had to pay rent for their own plot but the whole site was charged a nominal rent by colliery owners who very kindly put it in a contract that the rent was 'In perpetuity' which, much to the joy of the miners, is loosely defined as 'To continue forever.'

"Oil tell ya wat," O'Rearden was once heard to say, "some of them office wollers at the pit were as thick as friggin roofin trusses."

When it came to charging miners the coal boards administration team were often very benevolent or very shit scared of the mineworkers union because when it came to agreeing the rent was it was fixed 'In Perpetuity' at 1940"s prices and the contract said it couldn't be changed!

Twelve pound a year for a couple of acres of land and no-one complained, surprising really, as we all know how principled and honest miners are!

Of course the rent from each plot didn't reflect the generosity of the Coal Board, it more or less reflected the need to pay into the kitty for annual seaside excursions, best plot and biggest veg competition, hedge cutting and for water rates. Any surplus income from rents was held in reserve for some untold impending doom that would befall them though no one knew what or why they would need a reserve fund.

By far the most singular benefit to the allotment tenants was that the plots next to the pub and that gave every one of them the opportunity to nip in for a drink or an excuse to 'do a runner 'from the relentless tedium of being in sight and sound of 'she, or in these more liberal times he, who must be obeyed' on the grounds that they were duty bound to attend to their plot.

"Arm off to wata veg love" was often heard as the kitchen door slammed shut before any "wat agen?" response could be heard. There was no answer to the question so why bother to wait after all who needs a fight when you can have a drink with your mates!

"Ey up Windy, what's all that about?" asked O'Rearden.

Some 'barsteward' has told the landlord that they have seen slugs being thrown over the fence.

"Arr, well, its bin 'appening for years!"

"What?" Retorted 'Windy', "You mean it's true!"

'Gerra grip'.... of course it has, the 'ouses chuck "em in the allotments we chuck "em back or over here, depends where your plot is, Some of them slugs have got more flying hours in than the chuffin Royal Air Force!"

"Well, I hope you don't think that..."

"Yes you do Windy" interrupted O'Rearden. "Don't come the outraged 'toffy nosed gardener' with me I've known yuh too long."

"Why do yuh think yur stood in 'The Flying Slug' owd yuh think its gorrits name?"

Chapter 3

Mushy Peace

"Morning Mick"

"Morning Mushy, 'Ow ya dooin?" Replied O'Rearden.

"Can I 'ave a word, in me shed?"

"Arr, Course ya can." O'Rearden replied as he followed Mushy down the path to his shed.

Mushy Peace, like Mick O'Rearden had emigrated from Birmingham to Yorkshire some years ago.

O'Rearden did so as he followed his genitals anywhere and at that time they said "This Yorkshire bird is worth one" So he courted her, married her and moved north to Frighall so she could be close to her 'Mam'

"Me mam would like it here"
"But, she's been dead 20 years, this shopping centre wasn't built then, it wasn't even conceived then!"
"I know, but she'd like it here."

O'Rearden would shake his head at proclamations like this, he heard them all too often and often wondered would 'me Mam' ever say "It's shite here"

Mushy Peace on the other hand was, at the time of his departure from Brum, 'on the run.' "Oim a wanted man." He would tell those that listened to him.

Mushy had a penchant for garnishing his life with stories, so many stories that some thought he was over a hundred and ten years old when they added up the years he spent doing 'this and that'.

Most folk tended to accept that he was a nice old man who danced with the fairies and gave no cognisance to the fact that he might just be telling the truth!

Released from Winston Green Prison, following some time for setting fire to some 'rough bastards' business in revenge, he returned, to his home only to find his dad tell him to "scarper... they've bin lookin for yow!"

'They' were some 'hard cases' paid by the owner of a rundown garage that specialised in welding together, or 'ringing', two separate damaged cars to make one reasonably good looking car.

'Looks', in the second hand car trade, do not count for much when both parts of the car go their separate ways in the event of hitting too many road pot holes. And, it was one of these cars that Mushy had bought and had tried relentlessly to recover his money. Frustrated by the abject refusal to refund him and the threats of physical violence if he continued to pursue his claims, finally drove Mushy to park the cracked car across the garage entrance and then setting fire to the premises.

The parked wreck prevented the fire brigade from effectively reaching the garage but also identified him to the very people he wanted to wreak revenge upon.

So, scarper he did. For a while he walked the streets, and the pubs, of Birmingham, working for cash in hand, eating at the 'Sally Army' and getting a bath in one of the canals that once made Birmingham great.

It was at, or in, one of these canals that he met a tramp who was to transform his life by taking him in tow and showing him the 'ways of the road'. After a couple of years of sleeping rough, poaching and stealing, he arrived in Frighall.

Knocking on doors for odd gardening jobs with an ability to recognise plants, especially vegetables, he soon enamoured himself into the hearts of the locals. The fact that he had spent the last year or two so stealing from gardens and farms for a living completely escaped them... he was different!

As they headed towards the shed it seemed as if every two steps Mushy was saying, "These are me 'first earlies' these are me 'seconds', these are FI Savoy's, these are...

"Shut the fuck up an' gerrin ya shed. What's yow want me for?" Asked O'Rearden.

For many years O'Rearden had claimed, "There's only two 'Brummies' around 'ere and one of them makes me look good!" But, he had a lot of time for 'Mushy' Peace. He was a grafter and, despite his age, he wouldn't, or couldn't, say no to anyone who asked for help.

"Yow wanna cuppa, it's boiled, I were just avin one when I saw thee."

"Thee... thee!" what the fuck does that mean? I thought yow were a Brummie!"

"Shurrit, ar've ad this letter from Dolethorpe Council, its doin me ead in"

Mushy handed over a grubby letter marked to the 'Secretary of Frighall Allotment and Gardens Society'

Mushy had been elected unopposed, a story in itself, as the 'Lockie Sheriff' or to a post more professionally known as 'The Secretary'. For years he had carried out his duties with diligence and ensured that where there was non-compliance with the rules set by the National Coal Board, warnings were given, and then ignored! Even he used to quote 'rules are for fools, and laws are meant to be broken like yur mothers art!'

As time passed on and without any support from his committee, who only turned up at meetings if they were in 'The Flying Slug', He contented himself with going to his plot and shed every day accompanied by his faithful dog who spent most of the day listening to the command 'Gerreere.'

O'Rearden read the letter and asked, "What's up, they only want you to go to an allotment secretaries meeting?"

"Its dooin me ead in, why av I gorra goo to it? Ar've bin secretary for 15 years and never bin to a council meetin?"

"Cuz ar'kid... you're the Lockie Sheriff"

"Look ere, I've ad it, d'yow want the job? I ain't sleeping roight since I got this letter"

'It's a letter Mushy, it ain't a bleedin' threat, wot ya wurried about?"

"Bloody council, why they pokin their noses in a coal board allotment site for?"

"Cus r kid, the coal board disappeared over twenty years ago, yow needs to go an' see wot they want!"

"I ain't gooin, stuff em .... Will yow cum wi me?"

Challenged, O'Rearden had little option. He liked Mushy. He only had an allotment because Mushy bent the rules and jumped him up the waiting list.

"OK, tell me when it is, but we ain't gooin in your car it's full of dog hairs, we'll goo in mine. Remind me nearer the dreaded date!"

As he returned up the path towards his own plot, Mick's mind played havoc yet again.

There was old Arthur sat outside his shed but, Arthur had passed away, on that very plot, five years before! Mick watched Arthur raise his arm as if to wave but the arm fell off! "Bollocks," said Arthur, and, as he bent forward to pick it up his whole bedraggled frame fell forward into the ground where he had been found five years before.

I've got to stop thinking like this Mick thought to himself as the next spectre dressed as a pit worker doffed his damaged safety helmet in salutation.

"Ow do Bill, ows yur beans this year?" asked O'Rearden.

But Bill didn't answered, he never did. Bill was once again rushing to Frighall Colliery for the shift where a total roof collapse was to crush his skull and remove him from the list of plot holders. Unfortunately no-one had mentioned it to Bill and he came most days to tend his plot before rushing off to his fateful shift at the pit.

"You're going nuts O'Rearden," Mick said as he opened his shed after giving it a swift kick to frighten any mice inside.

Chapter 4

Striking a Happy Medium.

Mick put the phone down on the hall table and left the call centre worker talking away to herself while he went back to his ironing.

Once upon a time he would politely listen to the foreign accents and then, after thanking them for the call, he would hang up. Just lately it had become bloody nuisance with the number of calls he was getting, all which seemed to come from Asian sounding people who couldn't pronounce his name properly.
He learnt that if there was a short silence when he picked the phone up then an automatic dialler was waiting for the next available operator to pick the call up to give him the sales pitch. So now he'd just put the phone down and let them pay for the call.

"Hello Mr. Ored ann." "Hello can I speak with Mr Ore Edon."

"No you fuffin can't." Mick would say from the sanctity of the kitchen and out of earshot from the phone.

"Me name is O'Rearden and if yow can't pronounce it, yow dunt know me... so piss off!"

He used to answer, "Hello, Chief Inspector O'Rearden Regional Fraud Squad." Until he was told that impersonating a police officer was an offence. "Somebody ought to tell that to some of the buggers poncing around in uniforms at Dolethorpe cop shop." Mick had replied.

He had tried, "I'm sorry but the undertaker is here now removing Mr. O'Rearden remains." That was a sure fire way of getting them to hang up in silence. He stopped using that one when he thought that could be true one day and he just might be going 'feet first' out of the front door when the phone rang and he would miss an unrepeatable deal on double glazing, solar panels or even worse, miss out on making a huge saving on his own funeral costs.

Mick enjoyed ironing and had done so ever since the army introduced him to an iron and showed him how to press his uniform. Then it was a flat iron heated on a potbellied stove and shared with the other lads in the Nissen hut that was laughingly called a barrack room. Now it was an all singing, dancing and whistle blowing steam fangled thing that his late wife had bought him.

Mick ironed everything, "if it's bin in the washa it gets ironed... end ov" he used to tell people who questioned why he ironed his socks, underwear, towels and even dish clothes. He used to say he'd iron his wife's bra if he could get a wok small enough!

Ironing gave him escape, time to think and reminisce and remember how his wife always like pressed sheets and pillow cases with razor sharp creases but didn't like the same creases in her blouse sleeves.

I'll never understand bloody women, he used to think as she ranted at him.

 "Think yourself bleedin lucky yower ol man loikes ironin." he used to tell her.

 "And think theesen bleedin lucky I took thee in. Me mam said yud brek me art and tha dus it every day." His wife Josie used to reply.

She was never comfortable in hospital. The bed sheets, although pressed, were not the same as they were at home. They were pressed in some mechanical gizmo and they had 'Muxburgh Hospital' printed on them in sanitary blue ink. The pillow cases were flat with no creases and no amount of fluffing up would make them feel like someone cared. No one had ironed them after they had been hung out in fresh air and no one had come home from his allotment and picked up the washing to do the ironing so she didn't have to.

Mick Remembered how she'd laid in the hospital bed almost the colour of the sheets that she hated, and how, when he tried to make her comfortable, she chastised him for fussing.

"I carn't do roight fur doin wrong wi you Josie, you're looking all bovered, oim just tryin to mek yow comfy" Mick would say holding back the tears.

The doctors had told him it would be a matter of days before she passed and he had kept it from her.

"Doctors, fucking doctors, call yur selves fucking doctors, yur nowt but fucking body mechanics these days. At least wi mechanics some fucker up the road knows better and'll fix it for ya. You twats have been faffing about wi er for two fuckin years now and now you fuckin tell me she's terminal."

Before Mick had finished shouting an over-weight security guard resplendent in a uniform that stated 'I have no authority but I am large' appeared at the door.

"And yow can fuck off fatty afore I smack ya." Hissed O'Rearden. "My argument is with this tosspot ere but oil tek yow out wi him so get yur fat arse out of my sight"

Fatty took two steps back.

Leaning into the doctors face Mick whispered a threat, "Yow tell er she's terminal an' Yow'll die before 'er, is that fuckin clear. Yow shits ave failed her for long enuf now gie er some peace or by fuck yow'll answer to me."

Moving towards the door he said. "Shift ya fat twat and tek up joggin instead of pie eetin"

Fatty stepped back again.

He remembered how he stroked her hair as she lay slipping in and out of consciousness and he remembered the hours she had spent at home grooming herself before she went anywhere and that she would never leave home without 'a bit of lippy on'.

Now she was void of any colour, the sparkle in her eyes that had kept his love for her alive all these years was fast disappearing and his heart was heavy because she was sinking into the sheets she hated.

"Nurse, Oim teking er ome.... Mek the arrangements will ya?"

"I'm afraid she may be too weak Mr O'Rearden." The nurse replied.

"She'll be appier in er own bed, who do I see about taking er ome?"

The nurse went to fetch the ward sister and Mick went to take a quick toilet break. On his return to the bed the nurse was back along with the sister.

The sister looked and him and said softly "I'm afraid she has just passed Mr. O'Rearden."

"Bloody 'ell Josie, why dent ya wait for me tuh cum back, I've only been gone a minute." Fighting back the tears he picked up her limp hand, lent forward and kissed her.

"Is there anyone we can call?" asked the sister as the nurse pulled the curtains around the bed.

"No, there's only us two, we… we had a daughter but she died years ago, we wanted more but…"

"We'll leave you for a couple of minutes to say your goodbyes, I'll get a doctor and the hospital almoner to come and talk to you about the next steps." The sister said as she nodded to the nurse to leave.

Mick remembered the mind numbing haze that followed and leaving the hospital with a heavy heart and pamphlet that somebody had passed to him.

He remembered stopping at the allotments on his way home and going into his shed where he sat and cried.

The phone rang again bringing him back to reality. He picked it up ready to tell somebody in Pidgin English in they had phoned a Chinese 'take away'

"Mick, Mick, don't ang up it's me Tom"

"Eyup Tommy ow ya doin?" asked Mick glad to have a real caller.

"Mick we're off to Dolethorpe club tonight, there's a clairvoyant doing a show, do you fancy coming along? The missus is going to try to contact her sister, we thought you might want to come along to see if you ca…"

"Tom," Mick interrupted. "If Josie cud, she wud 'ave contacted me afore now, I dunt believe in that 'jiggery pokkery' but I'll come an ave a drink with yow and Mary".

Later in Dolethorpe Club and after the audience had sank four or five drinks and when the club steward knew they wouldn't buy any more until they were getting their monies worth and enjoying themselves… 'The turn' started his act.

"Is there anyone in here with a gardening connection?" The medium asked. "Anyone got any connections to gardening or perhaps allotments?"

"Av yow fuckin set me up?" Mick growled at Tom.

"No, no we ain't, honest Mick."

"There is someone in here who whiffs a bit of cow manure, somebody is wearing it as aftershave and not putting it on his rhubarb." The audience began to laugh and the medium, knowing laughter is infectious, played to his crowd and held his nose and said, "nar oo shure ders no one wi a gardun, phew shumeone pongs."

"Tommy, yow twat, if yow set me up I'll..."

"We ain't Mick, honest!"

"Oooh, it's here at this table I can see a smelly old gardener with a big thingy" The medium laughed as he pointed at their table. The audience, most of whom had known Mick O'Rearden for years, roared with laughter.

"What are yow laffing at?" Mick asked the medium.

"I can definitely see a smelly old gardener sat at this table"

Again the room erupted in laughter at Mick's expense.

A fist smashed into the medium face with a bone crushing thud. "And now.... yow can see fucking stars." Mick said.

As the medium crashed unconscious to the floor with blood spraying from his nostrils Mick turned to tell Tommy he was a twat when he saw a sallow faced ragged old bloke sat beside him holding an upright cucumber in his lap.

It wasn't until he was going out the door, having marched through the silenced audience that he realised what he had just seen. Turning, he saw Tommy and Mary helping the medium onto an empty seat and no one else. What he didn't know was that this was going to be the start of similar visitations. Striking a happy medium was going to haunt him, literally!

Chapter 5

Brenda Legges

One of the joys of being on the allotment in the early afternoon is watching Brenda. She may have been, the first and only woman to get an allotment plot at Frighall and she may have got it as a token to equality,   but when she was bent over weeding she became a bigger attraction than the Royal Family and was the cause of a lot of the other tenants coming for a chat with Mick who had the adjacent plot.

Brenda although now in her early 50's could fill a pair of jeans better than many women half her age and for the old farts working their plots it was a treat to admire her curvaceous figure from behind, from the side, from the front and from any angles they could.

"Brenda, stand up and use your hoe. The advance party from the Second Battalion of Dirty Ol' buggers is sneaking down the barrow path." Mick shouted a warning to her.

"Seen him Mick, That old soldier can't to stand to attention if you know what I mean" Brenda laughingly replied half turning towards Mick.

From that half turned angle she knew Mick would be able to see her in a fuller and more appealing side and knowing most men like breasts, posing half turned flattened her stomach and enhanced assets. Brenda had always held a candle for Mick and, since he became a widower, its flame burned more brightly.

Mick knew she enjoyed teasing the old blokes and 'Old Alan' walking towards them probably couldn't remember what he had come for let alone what he should do if he ever got the chance to sweep Brenda of her feet. Alan had become collectively known as 'Al Symer' for an obvious reason.

But Mick was more worried about the two blokes walking behind him. How could he tell Brenda that Alan was being escorted by the apparitions of two deceased plot holders? He couldn't even bring himself to discuss it with the doctor, let alone Brenda and what worried him the most was the thought that they too were coming to ogle Brenda.... do dead men still eyeball women, and if they are already stiffs ... what happens to the parts that used to get stiff?

"Ow do Mick, morning Brenda" said Al wiping his brow with snuff stained handkerchief. A lot of the ex-miners at Frighall allotments still took a pinch of snuff having become hooked on it when working on the coal face where all forms of smoking was banned.

"Oil Roight Alan, Ow ya doing? Do yuh need summat?"

"Morning Al" said Brenda leaning forward so the view of her cleavage was accentuated.

"Er, um, er.... Bloody ell what did I come to see you about, my bloody memory is getting shocking these days. What was it, erm?"

"Yow've walked less than 200 yards down the path and yow've forgotten what ya wanted me for! Maybe if you looked over ere at me yowed remember." Mick said.

"It was something our Len was saying"

"Your Lenny, ain't he got a plot over at Dolethorpe Council allotments?" asked Mick trying to kick start 'Al Symer's functioning memory cells. "What's 'appening over there, they aving problems?"

Turning on his heels and walking away, Al replied, "I'm buggered if I can remember... when I do I come back"

"Bye, Bye then Alan." Brenda said turning to Mick and saying "What's the betting on him returning?"

Brenda had the sun behind her causing Mick to squint as he looked at her silhouette. There was no doubt about it she did have a knockout figure when she held herself upright and there was no doubt that those dead buggers leaning on the fence were enjoying the view too.

Raising his had to shade his eyes, Mick replied, "e'll be back even if he dunt remember why or wot for." Then dropping his hand making a signal to the dearly departed that the show was over and that they should remain dearly departed and piss off, he asked Brenda if she'd like a cup of tea.

The kettle always boiled slowly when it was filled for two mugs and as Mick stood waiting for it he thought about the opportunities he had to get friendly with Brenda ever since she had arrived on the plot next to his.

Being new, he offered her advice and loaned her tools until she got her own and shared some of his unwanted seedlings with her. He enjoyed her smiles as she accepted his help, what man wouldn't. She was an attractive blonde divorcee with a wolf whistle figure.

Brenda wasn't your typical newly divorced woman. The very fact that she asked for an allotment must have given everyone a true insight to her real nature but she quickly became; "That 'Hussey' that's why tha wants to go to watta thee plants every bleeding night, tha thinks arm daft, What's she wanting an allotment for, can't keep a man of 'er own that trollop" and a lot of old boys heard it most days of the week after Brenda first arrived.

Mick enjoyed her company and had told his wife Josie about her arrival and about the conversations they'd had. Josie had never felt threatened by Brenda and when on the occasions they met she was comfortable chatting to her.

"There yow go Brenda, a cup of sergeant majors tea, strong and khaki lookin!"

"Thank you Michael," said Brenda as she cupped her hands around the steaming brew. "Just what the doctor ordered"

She pointed at an old bench at the top of her plot and asked, "Shall we sup in the sun?"

Mick enjoyed the view looking over his plot and he savoured the aroma of the freshly turned soil... well OK, he savoured the aroma of Brenda's closeness and the subtle hints of her perfume 'An Evening in Paris' or was that the scent his mom used? Whatever he knew he was sat next to a woman and it was nice.

For the first few minutes they sat in silence.

Brenda broke the ice and said, "I've been told there's Karaoke at 'The Flying Slug' next week, are you going?"

"Bluddy ell Brenda, yow nearly med me spill me tea... Ar of course oim going, oim gonna sing me favourite renditions of 'little ol tea drinker me' by Bean Fartin. No, I don't think I'll be there. How about you?" spluttered O'Rearden?

Brenda looked at Mick and said sadly, "I'd love to go but you know the wagging tongues around here, how could I go unaccompanied to any social functions without being a called a 'man eater?' I'd love to go though, I don't seem to go out much since he buggered off with his tart."

Mick suddenly felt the blame for her husband's dalliances, though he had no reason to. He was overwhelmed with an urgent desire to take Brenda to the pub and sod the consequences.

But more importantly… Alan was coming back!

"Ay yup Mick, Brenda. This is cosy sat in t'sun," said Alan. "I've just remembered what 'r'kid wur on about. Those twats at Dolethorpe Council are wannin them off so they can sell the land… or was it they wanna put the rents up or summat, Fukin ell I forgot again… It's a shit' deal eny ow!"

"Calm down Alan," Mick replied. "What yow on about? Slow down and tell us what your kid said."

Alan lifted his cap and scratched his head. "Mick, there's a meetin comin up and we're all gerrin shafted. 'R kid' is trying to muster up some elp tu feight em!"

"But why are yow tellin me?" asked O'Rearden.

"Cos," replied Alan. 'R kid said tell that "Brummie Twat" down your allotments!"

Mick looked at Brenda and shook his head, Brenda in turn laughed and said "Well at least he got part of it right, although I'm not sure if it's the 'Brummie' part or the latter!"

Chapter 6

Sundays Left Overs

Despite being alone, Mick sat at the dining table to eat his traditional Sunday Lunch. Josie had insisted that they sat at the dining table for every meal and Mick adhered to her ruling even now she had gone.

He still prepared Sunday lunch way as he had always done and Mick still used the same amounts. Josie's always made sure there was some left over for Mondays. Now it seemed there was enough left over for Tuesday, Wednesday and Christmas day

One of the benefits of an allotment was the abundance of vegetables that were available, the down side was he was still growing enough to feed the proverbial five thousand. Mick didn't really need the allotment nor the vegetables, he needed to escape the emptiness of the house and its memories.

Going to the allotments freed him from the sorrow he felt in his heart every time he opened a cupboard or a wardrobe. He knew he should have allowed a charity to take all her clothes and shoes and allow some less fortunate women to enjoy the envy Josie enjoyed when heads turned in admiration of the elegance and quality the clothes. But they were Josie's clothes and they were her enjoyment, her pleasure and his memories.

Since she departed Mick enjoyed a glass of beer with his meals, sometimes one or two more than he needed. After washing, drying and clearing away Mick sat in front of the very TV he hated and watched an old black and white movie until he could no longer fight off the 'full belly syndrome' which caused him to nod off.

The phone rang rudely waking him.

Not wanting to commit himself to answering whilst still half asleep Mick waited for the statutory call centre 'pick up' pause.

"Allo, allo…. allo can yow 'eer me?"

Happy that it wasn't a call centre and recognising the 'Brummie' accent' Mick said "Allo Mushy, what's up?"

"Mick, can I av a word?"

"Yur on the phone r'kid course ya can, what's up?"

"Wot's fuckin up….it's dooin me ead in that's fuckin wot! Ar lass sed I weren't t'bother thee t'day but ar can't sleep, I…"

"Calm down 'Mushy', calm down and tell me… why yow're phoning me on a Sunday, are the cops after yow agen?" interrupted Mick.

"No, it's this fuckin letta, that's doin me ead in!"

"Mushy, I told yow, it's a letter, stop worrying, I told ya I would come wi yow to the meetin"

"Oh are, but this un's different, it as come on Friday, an it's threatening us all wi eviction!"

"Wot are you on about 'Mushy', ave you been suppin the 'Scottish Nectar' again?"

"Mick, oy cannot sleep, 'onest, its doin me ead in, it sez we will foreclose your agreement and evict if……"

"Mushy mate, stop there, ask yur missus if yow can go to pub t'night, I'll meet yow there at seven, bring the letta!"

The Flying Slug was normally quiet on Sunday evenings, some would say that's how the gaffer would have liked it every day.

Sunday night regulars were usually the 'left overs' from Sunday lunch time who never adjusted to the new 'Open All Day' hours' and they mostly sat undecided as to whether they should actually go home and prepare for tomorrow's work or sit there and see if a free pint was in the offin!

Mick acknowledge their "ow ya doing Reardo?" and headed straight to the corner where 'Mushy' was sat.

"Don't buy me a drink Mushy I'll get me own, I usually av to when oim wi yow". "Where's this letta yows worried about?"

Mushy handed over a crumpled envelope.

"What as appened to this, as yower dog ad it?"

"No, oi chucked it in the bin when oi red it, its doing me ead in, loik I told ya."

"This is a different letter Mushy, and it's just a statutory notice tellin us the council's powers as our landlord."

It's only reminding us that if we dunt comply wi their rules or fall in arrears they can evict us, It's reminding us about a meeting this Tuesday…. What meeting on Tuesday, I thought yow wer gonna tell me when yow got the letter about the meeting?"

"Oi probably chucked it in the fuckin bin, oim sick them council twats, Never been in touch for years now all ov a fuckin sudden they're arassing me!"

"Stop wurryin, oyl phone em tommora an get the jist, then we'll go and see worrits about… an remember, we ain't gooin in that dog kennel car of yorn."

Mick offered to buy Mushy another drink but he declined so they both left. Mick didn't head straight home but instead walked towards the allotments. He thought to himself, 'I must be mad coming here this time on a Sunday evening'... but something compelled him to go.

As he turned the corner he felt sure he could see in the twilight, a torchlight beam coming up the barrow path that stretched the length of the site. Mick stepped into the cover of the overgrown hedge.

"Jesus Christ, Mick!" Shouted Brenda. "What the bloody hell are you doing down here. You frightened the life out of me."

"Sorry Brenda, luv, I dint expect anyone down ere, I just thought I'd av a walk to clear me ead"

As he spoke Bill passed them both.

"Night shift, is it Bill?" Mick asked before realising only he could see Bill.

"What?" asked Brenda?

"Sorry luv, just thinking out loud, oy told ya oy need me ead clearing. What yow dooin down ere anyway?"

"I came to light my paraffin heater, there's an early morning frost forecasted according to the television"

"Come on oyl walk ya ome" Mick offered.

"No, but you can buy me a drink, I've heard 'The Snug' is quiet on a Sunday evening"

"Where?"

The Flying Slug of course unless you'd prefer not to, I don't want to damage your reputation" Brenda replied coyly.

As they entered the pub the landlord turned to see who had dared come in his empty pub when he was hoping to close early now that the 'Sunday Left Overs' had gone.

Mick enjoyed Brenda's company but this was the first time he had been with her outside of the protection of the allotment fence and he was a bit stumped at what to talk about, she was after all the only woman he had been in the pub with as Josie never liked going drinking... Shopping for clothes, shoes or handbags, now that was a different matter.

Brenda found the common ground and broke the silence. "Have you heard any more on what Al Symer was talking about?" She asked.

"Well, there's a coincidence." Replied Mick, grateful that he had something to talk about. After half an hour their conversation was interrupted by the Landlord who, nodding towards the clock, asked if they wanted another drink.

Taking the hint, they left and Mick walked Brenda to her house.

"Oyl leave ya ere Brenda we dunt want your neighbours talking"

"Thanks Mick and thanks for the drink, it was nice. Maybe we could go to the Karaoke sometime now you and I have been seen in public"

"In public... There was only me and you in there!"

"And that miserable old bugger, he's is the biggest gossip in Frighall Mick, by Monday lunch the whole village will know... bye"

"Shit!" Thought Mick.

He walked home retracing their conversation to see if there was anything that could be misconstrued as a lovers tryst. He liked

Brenda but he knew she would never replace Josie. Though taken from him she still consumed his every waking moment. Now he felt he had let her down, he'd cheated on her, not just her memory but her. He couldn't have felt guiltier if he had an adulterous affair while she was alive.

Sleep didn't come easy that night.

Chapter 7

Our Lenny

As they pulled away from Mushy Pearce's house Mick said, "Listen Mushy, Ar've 'eard this meeting maybe a bit ov a stitch up. So shut the fuck up an let me speak"

"Why, wot yow eard?"

"Al Symer's brother as bin troyin to send messages to yow. But as usual 'Al' forgot who 'the real 'Brummie Twat' is!"

"Oy ent sayin owt, Oiv told ya its dooin me ead in."

Monday's phone call to Dolethorpe Council and a message left in the mailbox of 'The Allotment Officer' confirming the attendance of representatives from 'Frighall Allotment and Garden Society, was enough to ensure some tea and biscuits if nothing else.

Although, when he put the phone down, Mick couldn't help thinking.... 'Somebody is tekin the piss, an 'Allotment Officer' called Bernard Russel... come on... Brussel for fuck sake, Was his Mom and Dad Belgian? Or were his council mate's avin a laff when they said 'e was the best bloke for the job?'

Mick had thought it best to get some background information prior to the meeting so drove over to Dolethorpe allotments and found Al symers brother Len who looked like he was just about to leave.

"Ow do Len, Yur Al says yow been after Mushy Pearce but he got the wrong 'Brummie Twat' and ended up talking to me."

"Ey, I didn't mean anything by that." Apologised Lenny

"Don't wurry mate, no offence teken, Oive been call worse. What d'yow want with Mushy?"

"Come to the 'Rusty Dudley' with me I don't to say owt on here, too many arse licking snitches wanting a better plot from the council around here." Lenny suggested and nodded towards his neighbour's greenhouse.

"'E can't ear ya can e?" Queried Mick.

"I don't know but I reckon he can lip read, conversations I've had on here manage to get brought up at meetings before I raise them, come on I'm ready for a pint"

The 'Rusty Dudley' was full for a Monday lunch time especially as it didn't serve food. "Busy in here, is it normal?" asked Mick as they approached the bar.

"New landlord started today, so they're in for a traditional free pint, they'll piss off when they have to buy the next one." Laughed Len, who then suggested they sat under the painting of the now defunct Dolethorpe Pit.

Dolethorpe had been a prosperous town when the coal mine was open, now many of the shops were either boarded up or turned into charity shops. The new generation of workers drove to the plethora of call centres that had sprung up on the pit sites that abounded the area instead of walking or waiting for the pit bus.

It still managed to keep its seven pubs, two 'Working Men's Clubs' and ironically a 'Conservative Club' where the beer was amongst the cheapest and the clientele were mostly the very miners made redundant by the Conservative government. Whilst the picture of Her Majesty the Queen remained without a mark on it the same could not be said about the images of current and passed Prime Ministers!

"Look Len," started Mick, "Mushy Pearce is still the secretary but e's worried about wots gooin off. If owt is gooin off. Why av yow bin troiyng to contact im? I'm ere on is behalf as the old bugger is...."

"I'm glad you have Mick, summat is going off and I ain't sure it's for the benefit of us allotment members either." Interjected Len.

"That twat Russel has been showing people around our site, and they came in fucking a company car, fucking blazoned with their name 'Arsto Homes.' Now if that don't spell fucking dodgy, what does?"

Mick put his pint on the table and asked, "Is he for real, B Russel, is that his name or someone takin the piss?"

"Oh, he's for real all right," replied Len. "Small man... Big ideas. He wants to get on in the Council and has been putting forward ideas how to save or make money, none of the other council officers like him, he's up the arses of all the elected members and he needs their support when he puts in for jobs. The 'Allotments Officer' post introduced him to some prime building sites. Ours and your site fit that category. He is a twat of the old order. Selling off Council assets isn't just school playing grounds, it's us too mate!"

"But, allotments are designated by the Secretary of State as allotments and it's the law, the land can only be used as allotments," replied Mick. "Who's he kidding?"

"And the Secretary of State can 'un-fucking' designate anytime he fuckin wants, and that the problem.... Those twats in government have cut councils back because of 'austerity' so the Secretary of 'fuckin' State will agree so he and his mates aren't supporting us anymore and twats like Russel know that and see it as an opportunity for self fuckin promotion."

"OK", asked Mick, "What about this meeting?"

Len turned to Mick and said, "That's why I'm glad you've come and not Mushy, He's a nice old bloke but not what we need now, we need someone with balls to fight and I remember you at the pit.... never the quiet one!"

"Oh, Fuck," thought Mick. "What the fuck have I got myself in to?"

"Alroight Lenny, we'll tek it as it comes, I'll see what this twat 'Brussel Sprout' as to say, but oim up we yow, if only for the foight against the Council, I can't believe they would rob us lads… them councillors are ex-miners!"

"Yur right Mick, but they now have different paymasters…. the twats!"

Chapter 8

Dolethorpe Council

As they entered the Council Offices O'Rearden looked at Mushy Pearce and said, "Roight dunt forget, shut the fuck up an' leave it we me, Oyl do the talkin Yow do the cryin.. mek out yow've not 'ad any letters, just keep shtumm!"

True to his word 'Mushy' kept Shtumm, well almost!

The meeting on the other hand was an entirely different matter.

Opened by the 'Allotments Officer,' everyone was told about the statutory fire escape plan, everyone was asked to sign in, everyone was reminded who was in charge, him of course, and through whom comments should be made and how when making them they should identify themselves first and finally everyone was welcomed to the meeting.

"What the fuck," thought Mick. "We're as welcome as a fly in a web!"

"Shall we go around the table identifying ourselves?" asked Russel.

By the time it came to Mick's turn he had already nudged Mushy and declared himself the Chairman of Frighall Allotments and Gardens Society. Mushy duly declared himself as the Secretary and quickly asked why they had been invited when they had never been to a meeting before?

"We'll address that later shall we," came reply. The "WE" being emphasised by two fingers on each hand making quotation marks which made the reply mockingly condescending

"No," retorted O'Rearden. "I think 'WE' would like it addressing now so that 'WE' can decide whether 'WE' wish to take part in this meeting, as my colleague here says, this is the first meeting 'WE' have been invited to."

At every 'WE' his hand gestures copied those of the Allotment Officer who, not being accustomed to being challenged replied, "There is an agenda for this meeting and it has been posted to each secretary, and we should follow that agenda so we can properly minute this meeting."

"Is it," asked Mick, "beyond the wit and comprehension of your accomplice sat there, to make notes and then put them in order when typing the draft minutes for approval of all of us sat here, and surely an agenda should have the minutes of the last meeting attached to them?"

Suddenly this had become an interesting meeting and those who normally came to these meetings to listen to 'Ayatollah' Russel demand compliance with the allotment tenancy rules of Dolethorpe Council put down their tea cups and turned in their seats so they could hear better.

Len, sat opposite to most of the others, due to the chairs being arranged in the statutory council meeting 'we are all equal' format, looked at a couple of them and beamed a smile which confirmed 'What did I tell you'

"This young lady is not my accomplice nor do we have 'draft minutes' for approval, The minutes are typed and circulated before the next meeting so that comments or matters arising can be made at that meeting." Snapped Russel.

"What the fuck have I let myself in for, me and my bleedin big gob," thought Mick. "Here we go back to the old days, 'Joe fucking soap O'Rearden' getting into scraps on behalf of others who fucking keep quiet or run.

"By which time, most of us in here will have forgotten what was actually said or promised, and your colleague is the only person in the room not to have identified herself when 'WE' went around the table." Replied Mick gesturing the quotation marks again. "It is usual practice that before the final minutes of any meeting are submitted to the next meeting that 'those' present today can remind the young lady of what was said."

"I will reiterate what my colleague, the secretary of Frighall Allotments and Gardens Society has asked, why are we here when we have never been to a meeting before?"

"Over t'you" shouted one of the others around the table, "Ar cum on then, answer im" added another.

"Gordon 'Bennet' Jones, Muxborough Adick Street site, I would just like to point out that no-one from us site 'as been invited for over 6 years so like these lads... Ar want t'know what's appening, why av we bin invited?"

"Sit down Gordon, gie the lad a chance t'defend is sen" butted in Len adding, "If he can!"

Rising to his feet Russel addressed the meeting, "I have called you all here to tell you that following an audit of the Councils properties and estates, and due to the financial crash, allotment rents will be going up with effect from..."

"Not arn,' chirped up Mushy. 'Yow can't, an yow ain't got 'Frighall' chance!"

"Mushy," said Mick looking at him in the hope he would keep quiet.

"Dolethorpe Council, at its meeting on the 16th agreed that rents will go up and those in default will be regarded as such and tenancy agreements will be terminated 'en bloc'" said Russel looking smug.

Mushy stood up and said "Well, we'll see yow in court then." He picked up his papers and walked out.

O'Rearden was compelled to join Mushy, so he too gathered up…. Nothing… he had no papers, he didn't even have a copy of the agenda. "What the fuck!" He thought, what's the 'Real Brummie Twat' done now?" He looked at the Allotment Officer and his young lady accomplice who sat open mouth and said, " yow 'eard im we'll see yow in court" As Mick reached the door he was conscious of chairs being pushed back and people following him outside.

Mick turned and saw… did he see him or was his mind playing tricks again, 'Spud Murphy', No, it can't be he thought, why would 'Spud Murphy' be here? But he was being followed by most of the meeting.

In the car park Mick looked at Mushy who was heavily drawing on a cigarette. "What the fuck was that about?" he asked.

"Yow lot moight tek the piss but, we ain't council allotments we're Coal Board!"

"For fucks sake Mushy, the Coal Board disappeared years ago"

Thrusting his battered briefcase at O'Rearden he said, "Ere yow sort it out, I told ya oive finished, yow can ave it, its bin dooin me ead in."

"Old on Mushy" What the fuck are you on about?"

"I've resigned, yow can ave it, them's all the letters we av eva ad and not one of them is from Dolethorpe fuckin Council so they can't do fuck all."

The journey back to Frighall was, to say the least, a little tense. Mick tried to persuade Mushy that he shouldn't resign as he had been the best secretary the Frighall allotments had had in the last 15 years. That he needed to tell the committee first and hold a meeting to warn the other tenants of what was to come.

"Well yow can do that, seeing as ow yow elected y'self as chairman, there ain't bin another secretary in the last 15 fuckin years so shove yur praise up yur jacksie!"

"Mushy, let's call a meeting and see what the lads feel. The committee should be elpin ya, yow'll see they want yow to be the 'Lockie Sheriff', Oy'l tell em wots gone off and Oy'l gie em a bollockin for not supporting ya"

"Nowt tu do wi me, oive resigned, I told ya, its bin dooin me ed in and the chuffs are only on the committee for the glory... none of the twats ave dun out fuh years, so Mister fucking Chairman yow can call the fuckin meetin, cos I ain't"

As the car pulled up outside his home Mick looked across at Mushy and asked, "Is this what it's all been about, because I called me 'self the chairman, I did it on yur behalf because yow said it were dooin yer ead in?"

As Mushy got out of the car he leaned back in through the opened door and said, "Mick yows allas bin a gud mate, It ain't about you, It's me oyve ad enough. If oy ave to gie up mi plot oy will"

"For fucks sake Mushy no one has sed owt about giving up yur plot, Look oyl get a meeting called, yow come along and..."
Before he had finished Mushy had turned and walked to his front door. The only comment was a shouted "shurrup" to his dog that was barking from behind the window.

Chapter 9

Bloody 'Ell

Back Home Mick picked up the briefcase Mushy had left in the car and decided before anything else he was going to have a whisky, he needed that if nothing else and now Josie wasn't here to remind him of his excesses he made it a large one.

Mick was glancing through the contents of the battered briefcase and thinking about the shambles of a meeting he had just attended.

Silly old fart, why did he kick off when he did? We had 'Brussel Sprout' on the back heel.

Fancy seeing 'Spud Murphy' I wish I had had more time to talk to him, thought Mick.

He and 'Spud' had been good mates at the colliery but like all male friendships they drifted apart when 'Spud' moved to another pit instead of taking redundancy...."I've got young uns Mick, I need to work, to put bread ont' table."

As Mick picked up a yellowing documents he said "Bloody Hell, Jeez, Ol' Mushy is right."

The document may have been faded but it was clear what it said.

Head of Terms of Agreement dated this day 20th December 1947

An agreement between The National Coal Board hereinafter referred to 'The Coal Board' and The Frighall Allotments and Gardens Society hereinafter referred to as 'The Tenants'.

All the lands that are contained within fields shown on the Ordinance Survey map SE 601421 and SE 441821 amounting 4.665 acres, shown on the attached map, coloured pink and lying within the Parish of Frighall the ownership of which shall be transferred to 'the Tenants' subject to 'the Coal Board' maintaining all mineral rights, wayleaves and easements

The tenancy shall be determined by either party giving to the other party not less than 12 calendar months' notice in writing of either parties intention to cease trading or acting thereof as a business or society."

'The Tenants shall …

"Shall be transferred to 'The Tenants'" Mick said again and again.

"Shall be transferred to 'the friggin Frighall tenants."

The remnants of his glass of whisky had barely passed his throat before Mick was on the phone to Mushy Peace

"Mushy mi ol mate, oy reken yow were roight it's ere in the…"

"Hello Mick" said Mrs Pearce. "I'm afraid Peter has gone to bed, he said he wasn't feeling too well and, he hasn't slept well lately worrying about the meeting, I'll tell him you called when he gets up."

"Peter?" Thought Mick, "all these years and I never knew he was called Peter."

"Thanks Beryl, I'm sorry I disturbed you, tomorrow will do"

The rest of the agreement contained the rules of tenancy and the clause about the rent which specified that £12 must be paid every 12 months in two instalments and that the rents would be fixed at that rate until mutually agreed by both parties.

"Office wollers… Thick as fuckin roof trusses all roight." Laughed Mick.

He read and re-read the agreement. There was no mistaking it the land had been transferred to the society, it belonged to them. The Coal Board had ceased trading in 1994 when it was privatised and no notice of intention to cease trading had been given... or had it?

Mick emptied the contents of Mushy's battered briefcase on the lounge carpet.

"Sorry Josie" he said, looking up, when he realised that not only were there old documents but what seemed like half a ton of allotment dirt and tobacco bits. "I'll Hoover it up love.... Just as soon as I have read this lot.

Mick grabbed the whisky bottle and sat on the floor next to the jumbled pile of letters and notes. He hadn't felt like this since he took on the job as a union rep at the colliery. This was something he used to love, preparing for a meeting against unprepared managers.

Having the ammunition to counter their suggestions, which invariably was about saving money and increasing profits, and having your own evidence to blow them out of the water in support your case which was always the opposite of what they wanted.

First things first, chronological order then... No, first another whisky!

When Mick tried to stand after sitting on the floor for two hours he didn't know whether it was old age and cramped muscles or the whisky that made him struggle.

He had managed to put all the old notes, letters and minute books into some sort of chronological order and briefly read each of them as he did so. Despite there being many gaps between communications it was evident, Dolethorpe Council had never communicated with them before the invite to the meeting that he had brought to an abrupt end.

Better still, he was now armed with a tenants list, complete with their contact details though he wasn't sure how many still had plots nor how many occupied plots up at Frighall cemetery!

He decided his priority was to call the committee members and to let them decide what they wanted to do as they represented the tenants of Frighall Allotments and Gardens Society.

Chapter 10

Frighall Allotments Committee

"Committee? Am I still on the committee, I thought I had packed in years ago!" Seemed to be the general reply to each call, or "Committee? We haven't had a meeting in years, never been anything to discuss!"

"No, you are still on the list, and I'm phoning to tell you I have something important to tell you, you need to hold a committee meeting as soon as possible."

"Why are you phoning Mick? Why hasn't old Mushy Peace called … he's the secretary?"

"Mushy isn't well, but he'll be at the meeting, I've called because I have some news for everyone but it needs to come via the allotments committee."

After calling five of the 'alleged' committee, Mick decided that they were 'RHINO's in that they were 'Really Here In Name Only' volunteers and only there for the protection and perks the status gave them.

Members of the illustrious committee always seemed to escape the annual plot inspections and were always the first ones to remove the contents of any value from vacated sheds, greenhouses and plots.

None of them had been of any support to old Mushy in the last fifteen years... not that he would have asked any of them for assistance. "I wouldn't call them twats for 'elp if 'oi' were on fuckin fire and... if it were them that wos on fire, I wouldn't piss on any ov them!"

Next morning Mick decided to pop round and see if Mushy was feeling any better and if he was fit enough or willing to come to a meeting.

"Peter, its Mick O'Rearden, come to see you." said Beryl as she ushered him into the lounge.

"All Roight Mushy, Ow ya dooin mate? Asked Mick.

"Oim ballaxed Mick, Oi ain't bin roight for weeks now, not since the fuckin letters come from Council, wot the fuck do they want wi us?

"Ey up mate... Stop worrying, yow were roight, its fuck all to do wi them, oive read all the stuff in the case yow left in me car. I reckon we should ave a committee meeting and then a tenants meeting....."

"Stop there Mick, oive finished, oive ad enough ov it and ar lass agrees, they ain't bin bovered for God knows ow long, so the twats ain't gonna elp us now!

"Come on Mushy yow were always up for a fight wiv the gaffas at the pit, Oi thought yowed be ready for a scrap"

Beryl came in with a tray laden with mugs of tea and homemade scones.

"Mick, I don't want him upset again, He's finished as secretary and it won't be long before he has to give up his plot."

"He has grown some lovely stuff and fed us, and nearly everyone else on this street during the miners' strike, now he struggles to carry the veg home."

"These letters from the council have upset him and really set him back. He's 82 Mick, it's time he stepped back and let them buggers who were happy to let him run it for fifteen years have some responsibility."

"OK, Oi suppose oi know Beryl, Oi was just tryin to give im a bit ov spark back, yow know we've bin mates for years an we ad some shit slung at us when we were union men at the pit."

"Yes Mick, but he was younger then and, a bit of a devil, but he's slowing down, let us have rest from him worrying."

"OK Beryl, any more tea in that pot?"

Mick spent close on to an hour reminiscing with Mushy. He enjoyed chatting about old times but saddened that his 'Old Mucker' was no longer up for the fight. As he had suggested to Beryl, he wanted to put a bit of a spark back into his mate, he wanted to see him front up to his enemies, to challenge them and say "Goo on, Oi dare ya."

Beryl was right, Mushy had suddenly become old and weary, now it was telling on him. His memory of past events were not as accurate as Mick's and he wouldn't be up for any fight.

Mick said his goodbyes with a promise to be back soon and then walked down the garden path to the sound of Mushy shouting 'shurrup... gerreer' to his dog.

Back home Mick decided to change tack.

"Hello its Mick O' Reardon, Oim callin on behalf of Mushy Peace he wants yow to 'old a committee meeting at 'The Snug'... Yes The Flying Slug... next Wednesday at 7 pm. No, his phone has been cut off, roadworks outside or summat, OK see you there then."

Just five of the committee members agreed to turn up. Whether it was a genuine interest or just a desire to get out of the house and into the pub no one could guess until the meeting commenced... or, didn't!

Chapter 11

Sid Davis

The clock behind the bar had already passed 7pm when Mick ordered his second drink. Believing some of the committee would turn up early he had himself arrived 30 minute early only to find that he remained alone apart from the landlord and he was only there because he lived upstairs.

"What you doing here tonight Mick, don't usually see you in here midweek and this early. Is something going off?" asked 'Droopy'.

Like his pub, the landlord have been given a nickname which was in homage to the 'brewers droop' the age old symptom of drinking too much beer!

"Yes Gaffer, we're supposed to be holding a 'Lockie' committee meeting here at 7 tonight looks like I'm it!

"A committee meeting" Laughed the landlord. "There ain't been a meeting in here for the last... 10, maybe 20 years and then half of them got so pissed they fell out with each other!"

The door opened and in walked Marty, one of the allotment tenants. "Bloodycowd innit?" He said rubbing his hands together, "Alright Mick, alright Droop...gissa a pint gaffa. I'm gagging."

Marty was built like the proverbial brick shithouse. Tall, strong and with a weather beaten face that showed, as a bricklayer, he would have, over the years, built one or two shithouses, though his bosses would have preferred them to be call 'Forever Homes.'

Mick liked him. He was brusque and not afraid to speak his mind, couldn't care less who he offended but... he was someone hadn't got the heart to kill off his old hens when they stopped laying. He let them die of old age... if the foxes didn't get them first.

"Ey up Shyler." replied Mick. "Are you busy?"

"Wages are still coming in Mick, but they want us to work all hours and every day for fuck all."

"What's happening in Dolethorpe? Word has it there's the chance of some development around there?" He replied as a pint of beer drained instantaneously down his throat. "Stay there and get me another gaffa, that didn't touch the sides."

"What's this then?" Mick asked attentively.

"We've been told, by the directors, to hold on if we were thinking of moving on as something big is going to happen around here. They won't say anything more, but that some local work may be in the 'offin' and it may be big... a couple of local sites they reckon."

Mick was about to ask more when in walked the first of the committee members.

"Find out what you can Marty, and let me know on the QT please" asked Mick holding his finger to his lips to emphasis secrecy.

"Why, is summat goin off?"

"I'll tell you another time mate, I just need some info about these sites, before anyone else if I can."

"There is no more, it's probably just our bosses trying to stop us from being poached on to other firms, and they'll have made it up." Laughed Marty.

"Find out what you can mate."

Both members of the committee who came in nodded at Mick and waited at the bar to be served.

Another committee man arrived, ignored the others and blustered his way up to the bar.

"We'll be better off in the Concert Room." suggested Mick.

Once they were seated Mick opened "Well its half past seven, do you think we will get anymore?"

"Not worth it Mick, we're not even quorate. What's the problem and where's old Mushy I thought he called the meeting?' queried Bryan Parkin. Bryan shared a plot with his mate Colin Stane who was sat beside him with a glass of rosé wine.

"Mushy ain't too well, but I know what he wanted to tell you as I went to an allotment meeting at Dolethorpe Council with him." Mick replied.

'Tha shut the fucking meeting down as I've 'eard. Tha were a gobshite at pit an' thar's not changed be all accounts. Who elected you as fucking chairman….Theesen… not us ont committee nor any of the tenants? Thar just poking thee fucking nose in creating bother like tha allus did." Sniped Sid Davis.

Sid had long been an adversary of Micks ever since Mick, as union man, refused to help him when he was caught stealing.

He was a 'Blackleg' who had broken the strike and returned to work. Despite having a wage he went shop-lifting and when caught he sobbed an excuse that he was on strike with no money to feed his kids. Most of the shopkeepers were sympathetic and let him off, after taking back their goods… All excepting one who knew him as a 'scab' and called the police… who just happened to have some picket line scores to settle with striking miners.

Denied legal support from the Mine Workers Union, he was fined enough to take away the gains he had made by going back to work and, with his picture plastered all over the local newspapers, he was known by all the shops and ostracised by everyone in the mining community.

He hated Mick with a vengeance!

"Well Mr. 'Fucking smart arse' Chairman, thar's not got a committee because I've phoned them and they've all resigned."

"We haven't." Interjected the two others who had sat quietly waiting for the meeting. "We would like to hear what Mick has…"

"Mr and fucking Mrs, what the fuck has anything got to do wi you two arse bashers, thar's only got an allotment for the shed… We all know what you get up to, 'if the shed's a rocking don't come knocking'… couple of wankers"

Mick stood up and leaned into the face of Sid Davies and said, "Yow really are an obnoxious twat."

"Every fucker knows yow've always had a grievance with mi, so cos yow ain't got the balls to tackle me up front ya goes beyind moin, everyone's back, to stick the knoife in. Well ya fat lump ov shit…. yow ain't got at me but yow probably destroyed the whole fucking allotments and the pleasure of a lot of men in the village, but then yow've got some 'istory for doing that."

"Fuck Off" replied Davies as he stood to leave.

"You fuck off fatty, we haven't resigned, and we want to hear what Mick has got to say." Said the youngest of the two whose nickname had been 'Coleen' for years. Me and Bryan are sick of your insults, you're lucky we haven't sorted you out before now, isn't he Bry…"

"Sort me out… sought out my arse more like…"

With that Bryan launched punch fairly and squarely in Davis's fat belly sending him falling back into his chair. Had Bryan been standing, he would have hit Davis in the face and blackened at least one of the eyes that now stared back in disbelief.

"If oi were yow, I'd piss off now before ya upset him." Laughed Mick. "Wait while this gets around, Oi can't wait tu tell everyone. Fat arse gobshite Davis has been knock down by 'Bry Anne' cos he insulted 'Coleen'. Yow'll never live it down…. Now piss off"

As he walked through the door, Davis turned and said "You'll live to regret that O'Rearden."

Mick ignored him and looked at the Bryan and Colin who was massaging Bryan's hand. They looked and said "Well, we're 'Parkin and Stane right here', what do you want us to do they." said in unison. 'Parkin and Stane right here' was their catchphrase and they loved to say in an effeminate way as they waved with floppy wrists.

They had been a couple for so long that only strangers had any doubts about their relationship and most everyone who knew them accepted them as they were.

"Well as you two are the only committee men here and as you pointed out, the meeting ain't quorate. The only thing I can ask is that you call an Emergency General Meeting of all tenants as we need a committee, with a chairman, secretary, and a treasurer."

"Leave that to us Mick, we'll write to everyone and make some posters to put up in the village. Do you think 'Fatty' will want to come?" Winked Colin.

As Mick walked home he watched moths batter themselves against the street lighting.

"That's me 'Icarus Mickarus', yow were roight Josie," he thought. "I throw meself into the fire every bleedin toime"

He remember Josie asking "Ow come its allus thee that's teking the gaffers on. How come none of the other chuffs want to fight for their sens?"

"I suppose it's me nature Josie, I dun't like to see people being taken advantage of just cos they ain't got the balls to speak up for th'sens, a lot of them have kids and debt so they keep their heads down. We ain't so…"

As soon as he said it he wished he'd kept his gob shut.

Josie was wounded and when Josie was hurt by comments about children she went quiet.

"Come on luv, Yow know wot I mean…. I din't mean to hurt your feelings."

"Icarus bleedin Mickarus, tha as tu bring it up every time. Thar wants the bright lights of union fame, help thee mates out and get a pat on the back… but once again tha as to remind me that I failed you" with that she stormed out of the room.

"Josie luv, I din't mean owt." It was too late. Josie was upstairs and crying.

Mick remembered how happy they had been at the birth of their daughter Rose and the joy she had brought them. Sadly at the age of three she was taken from them.

Little Rose was born with congenital heart disease as a result of Josie contracting German measles during her pregnancy and Josie never forgave herself.

No amount of consoling by Mick and her family would convince her it was not her fault.

The phone rang and brought Mick back to reality, he was back home and sat with a drink, which he probably didn't need but it comforted him when he thought of the two most important people in his lie.

"Hello Mick, its Brenda. I hope you don't mind, I'm just being nosey and wanted to know how your meeting went."

He really wanted to say "Not now Brenda." But he couldn't. She didn't know he was feeling remorseful.

"Well three turned up and I was told by Sid Davis that the rest had resigned and that we ain't got a committee because of me!"

"You're joking."

"Nope, he's bin shit stirring. Yow know what he's loike. E's phoned em all up and told them I ad appointed meself as Chairman, which is partially true but, it wur on a temporary basis to help old Mushy."

"I've asked Parkin and Stane, as the only two who ain't resigned, to call an emergency tenants meeting so I'll tell everyone wots appened then."

"If you need help Mick you know you can call on me." Brenda offered.

"Thanks luv, I'll have a chat wi yow tomorra wen I've ad chance to get mi ead round it a bit!"

"OK Mick, it's late we'll chat down the allotments, good night love."

Alone again with his thoughts he pondered on the events following Rose's death. How Josie could barely talk to him and how she spent hours in the baby room he had decorated for the 'sweetest rose' in their lives. He remembered how he had to go to the allotment to cry so that he appeared strong for Josie but all she did was accuse him of not caring and how she couldn't see that her accusations were just ripping apart his broken heart.

The day of the funeral most of Frighall had turned out to mourn as the hearse passed by and now no amount of anti-depressants could keep Josie together as she saw the solemn faces of friends and neighbours, many wiping their tears, peering at the hearse carrying her baby. By the time the committal was completed, Josie was a sobbing wreck.

She said. "When tha thinks tha can't cry any more tha dus." Those words came back to haunt Mick at Josie's funeral when he felt just as bereft.

As he lay in bed other words played on his mind… "You'll live to regret that O'Rearden."…. He'd been threatened!

Chapter 12

New Committee

"Well, we think you'd be a good chair, and we recommend to everyone that you are elected first, so you can pick your own team." suggested Colin Stane as he looked across to Bryan who nodded in support.

"As your only committee members we recommend Mick O'Rearden as chairman, any objections?" Asked Bryan Parkin.

"Yes, I object and so does everyone else who remembers 'im from pit." shouted none other than Sid Davis from the back of the crowded room.

Parkin and Stane had done as they promised, all the tenants had turned up for the meeting and a lot were accompanied by suspicious wives who had long suspected that these meetings were just an excuse to visit the pub.

Heads turned to see who had objected.

"Aye, an we remember thee from pit." Came a response.

"Tha not kiddin, I remember who the biggest chuff were an it ain't O'Rearden." shouted another.

Sid, it seems still had history.

"Look, we'll have to have a show of hands, who's in support of Mick O'Rearden as chair of the new committee?" Asked Bryan as Coleen stood to count.

"It looks overwhelming in support but can I please point out that only paid up tenants show hands, visitors are not allowed votes."

"That's thirty two in support, now those who object please show hands." Two hands were raised. "Mrs Davis, can I reminded again that only paid up tenants can vote… That's one against then, thank you."

"Point of order please' shouted 'Old Windy'. 'We should ask if there is anyone else willing to stand."

"Thank you Mr Millar, that's a good point, is anyone else willing to stand as chair?" asked Coleen?

"Are me, I'll stand." Shouted Sid Davis.

"Ok, can we have another show of hands, who is in support of Mr Davis as chair?" Again two hands shot up. "Mrs Davis, I'm sorry but you really cannot vote. That's one for himself, now those against please… Well, that certainly is overwhelming."

"Tha's counting everyone, wives and all and…'im, he's only collecting the fuckin empties!"

"Oh, why don't you just shut up?" Sniped Sid's wife to rapturous laughter.

"Well Mick it looks like you're our new chairman, do you accept?" asked Bryan.

"Off course 'e will, beers are on O'Rearden." Shouted Marty Shyler.

Mick looked around the room and thought. 'Is it only me who realises that there are more tenants in here than we have plots?' Did it matter that some of them had long since taken up a plot up at Frighall church yard? Did it matter if they weren't included in any head count? "Well,' thought Mick. "The least you could say I was 'dead' lucky to be voted in."

Bryan Parkin accepted the role of Secretary when nominated by Colin Stane and was proposed and seconded. Brenda Legge was voted on as treasurer. Mick, knowing the relationship between Chair and Treasurer had to be close, wasn't too pleased and neither were a lot of wives given the humphing and tutting they made.

The request for committee members was met with a proposal for Colin Stane 'See, we really are 'Parking and Staying'... on the committee." Coleen added once the vote was confirmed. No one else raised their hands, so Brenda suggested Windy Millar and Martyn Shyler both of whom accepted once goaded by the audience.

'I'll give it a go, if no one objects.' A chap at the back stood up and said. 'I know I am a bit of a newbie, but if no one else is prepared to stand, I don't mind helping out until we are established. My name is Walter Watt, I've only had a plot for about 7 weeks now?"

Almost immediately someone asked "What's 'is name?"

"Yes!" Came a reply.

Only to be met with "is names not Yes...its Watt."

"Yes it's Watt."

"Tha what?"

"No, 'Tha Watt, were 'is fatha."

"OK, OK." Intervened Mick, "I think 'Tha Watt' yow've just got yourself a nick name."

Once Walter had been proposed, seconded and voted in Mick said, 'we have one more vacancy on the committee and I'd like to propose Sid Davis, can I have a seconder please?'

A cacophony of moving chairs as people got up to leave drowned out Sid Davis saying, "Tha allas was a cocky twat, I'm not finished with thee."

"With no seconder then, I like to propose that Mushy Peace remains as a committee member."

"I'll second that." shouted four different voices from the exit door, followed by someone shouting "Anyone against…carried!"

As Mick stood at the bar buying the new committee a celebratory drink, Marty Shyler asked, "What the fuck were that about, proposing that pillock Sid Davis?"

Mick replied. "I'd sooner have him inside the shed pissing out than have him outside the shed pissing in."

The memory of Sid Davis saying, "I'm not finished with thee," walked home with Mick O'Rearden that night. 'Oive bin challenged again… bring it on!'

Chapter 13

Brussel Sprout

The following morning's phone call to Dolethorpe council to inform them of the changes to Frighall Allotments committee gave the new secretary Bryan Parkin a surprise.

"Thank you for your call, but we have been advised that we should refer calls from your society directly to Mr Russel office"

"Why's that then?" asked Bryan.

"I'm sorry sir, but I don't know. Mr. Russel is unavailable at the moment. When you phone back can you ask for his extension directly...? You will get him on 1,2,1,2."

"1, 2, 1, 2. 'Whitehall 1, 2, 1,2' was the old cops number for Scotland Yard, who does he think he is?" asked Mick as he agreed to phone Russel about the changes.

"You're through to the number of Mr. Bernard Russel, I'm sorry I am out of the office at the...."

The answering machine was interrupted by, "Hello, Mr. Russel's phone, this is Tracy his administrator, how can I help you?"

"Ello luv, this is Mick O'Rearden, oim phonin to tell yow about committee changes and contact details for Frighall allotments."

"Hello Mr. O'Rearden, this is Tracy, I think we met at the last allotment secretaries meeting. I was taking notes... in my 'conspiratorial way...'

"Oim sorry about that Tracy luv but 'e were winding me up."

"Well you're not alone there!" Wasn't the reply Mick expected?

"My grandad had one of your allotments, Percy Grover, everyone called him 'Percy Thrower', don't know why, did you know him, he passed away years ago?"

Mick wanted to lie and say he knew him but bottled out and said. "Before my toime luv but all the old lads talk about im."

"You all need to be careful, Mr. O'Rearden, There are a lot of things changing and not all for the good, I can't say more at the moment but please tell me the changes to your contact details and I promise to keep you in the loop."

"Where's Russel then?" asked Mick.

"He's meeting someone called Sid Davis who phoned this morning…"

'Wham, bam and thank you mam' thought Mick, 'the plot thickens!'

"Do me a favour luv, tell im oive called to notify yow of the changes and that oive asked that all communications for Frighall allotments are directed solely to me, and… do yourself a favour, don't mention telling me about Sid Davis."

Mick poured himself a whiskey and thought, what's his game, why is Davis having secret meetings with the 'Brussels Sprout'? He also thought about why he had poured the drink and how since Josie had passed no one was chiding him on the number of drinks nor the size of measures he was having.

"Do I tell the committee or keep it to myself? Would it be wrong to keep them in the dark while letting them get on and run the society, what if it went 'tits up' and they were held responsible?"

He had pretty much made up his mind to call his old mentor Mushy for a chat when the phone rang.

"Hello Mr. O'Rearden, this is Bernard Russel, I understand that you have been trying to contact me and that you want all communications for your society to come to you."

"Yes, that was why I phoned the authority but for some reason all calls about Frighall Allotments must go to you directly."

"That's correct Mr. O'Rearden, however your request is a bit unusual as normally the Authority deals with allotment secretaries or treasurers."

"It's no more unusual than our society having to come directly to you.... can you tell me why that is Mr. 'Allotment Officer'?" Replied Mick.

"I understand that you are all new in post, so I thought it may be wise to guide you through the Authorities procedures until you are on your feet."

"Thank you," Mick fired back. "But under the Authorities procedures everyone is to be treated equally so unless you are personally guiding every society in the area I suggest you leave us to our own means, and having been notified that all communications come through me, I further suggest that you notify all your departments of our request. Lastly can you tell me how you know we are all new in post when the calls to notify you were made this morning after our society meeting last night?"

If pauses could have babies the one that followed was certainly pregnant ...

"Err, it's totally unnecessary, but have it your own way Mr O'Rearden, I look forward to your calls for help." With that Russel hung up.

"And I look forward to your calls for mercy... Pillock! Thought Mick as he redialled Mushy Peace's home number.

"Hello Beryl, its Mick O'Rearden, how's Mushy... err, Peter doing, is he any better?"

"Hello Mick, He's coming along nicely... are you going to come and see him, it would cheer him up?"

"If yow av any of them scones ready oy'll be around in two shakes of a rag man's rattle."

"I'll have some ready by tea time Mick, are you coming today?"

"Tea time it is then Beryl, oy'll bring ya some veg."

A chat with his old mate didn't relieve his concerns about keeping the committee informed of the subterfuge but Mushy reminded him how he as secretary struggled for years without support and carried the burden and the blame for anything and everything.

A quick call to the others and a meeting was arranged and, it was to happen at his home.

He wondered what would Josie think, after the initial 'Tha better tell them to tek their boots off, I don't want allotment muck on my floors.' He resolved she'd probably be welcome of some guests so she could do her hair up, make a fuss and then be the victim who had to clean before and after they had been, although not at all necessary.

Chapter 14

War Cabinet Meeting.

"Come in, tek me as yow find me," Mick repeated as each of the team arrived.

Brenda arrived armed, not only with the accounts, but also a foil covered tray full of sandwiches.

She was followed by Marty suitably equipped with a case of beer, "ands off they're mine," he winked.

Bryanne and Coleen traipsed through the door and quickly scanned the surroundings noting colours, curtains and cushions. "Time for a makeover." Coleen whispered and was then promptly stabbed in his back by the top of a bottle of Rosé wine and given a threatening 'Shush'

The newbie, Walter 'Tha' Watt, came last and to the astonishment of the others, he came carrying a brief case!

"Windy Millar, ain't coming he's got a Parish Council Meeting tonight." Announced Colin.

"I din't know he were on the Parish Council"

"Yes." Replied Marty. "His missus told him he had to, status, I think."

As the tea service was returned to the kitchen cabinet and was being replaced by glasses, Mick said quietly to Josie "They all wiped their feet love and yes, I'll hoover up when they go." By the time he returned to the lounge the room was filled with laughter.

His "can we have some order please?" Was met with "as thee any Prosecco or gin?"

Suitably briefed, albeit without the machinations and treasonous behaviour of some, Mick let the meeting change from a full blown 'War Cabinet' with each of the committee briefed about their new roles and objectives into an enjoyable soiree.

Brenda fussed and competed with both Bryanne and Coleen to serve and to clean up, Marty took advantage of 'they're mine' and supped the lot.

Walter, sat quietly, until he finally succumbed to a very large glass of Mick's whiskey, whereupon he decided he needed more guidance on his 'brief' and asked could he come back when his head was clear only to be given another glass full and a pat on the back from Marty who for good measure assured him he was a 'Decent Twat' just like his father.

Brenda had already begun making suggestions about how they could increase the 'war funds' and was prompting Coleen and Bryanne, as joint secretaries, into making some posters. She had already suggested raising the tenants' rents from their historic ten pounds a year and was asking Martyn, the newly appointed Vice Chair if they could shorten some of the empty plots into smaller more manageable sizes to encourage more women to take up a plot.

"More women?" gasped Martyn. "We'll be 'aving cushions and curtains in the greenhouses next!"

"Not a bad idea." Walter interrupted. "The council will be wanting to see our equal opportunity policy, so if we can prove that we're taking all the necessary steps to encourage more diversity…. I'll write something into the new rules."

"Don't forget to include a health and safety policy, it'll be a help to Martyn when he's bollocking tenants about the state of their gardens" Bryanne quipped.

"I like the bollocking bit, can I start with that pillock Davis?" Grinned Martyn.

"No." Said Mick. "We need to notify everyone about our new rules and everyone will have to sign their acceptance.... Then you can start with Sid Davis"

"And those that won't sign?" asked Bryanne

"We will tell them that as we are now being managed by Dolethorpe, we need to comply with all their allotment policies and as such if they wish to keep their plots they will have to accept the new rules."

Mick knew who the first one to disagree with the changes would be but he was confident that Sid Davis would sign to keep his plot so that he could report back to Russel.

"What about old Mushy?" asked Martyn? "What's his job, the poor old bugger?"

"Mushy can be a mentor to new tenants, I was thinking that his plot will be the first one to be divided up and that he can share mine, until he is ready to pack in." suggested Mick.

"He'll be a help to me as I need time to get round the other allotments and agree tactics with their committees as to how we tackle Dolethorpe Council."

"I think you're beginning to enjoy your new job." Brenda commented.

Mick heard Josie saying. "New job? It's what he's always done... He's always carried the banner for every other bugger, he's only happy when he's fighting the bosses"

As they started to leave Mick suggested that there was a need to have more regular tenant's meeting at the Flying Slug and that prior to them, committee meetings could be held at his house again.

"Parkin and Stane will have a newsletter out by the end of tomorrow." said Coleen as they waved goodbye from the garden gate.

"And I'll have a draft constitution and an up to date set of rules and guidance notes by Friday… compliments of Google." Promised Walter.

As he left Martyn broke wind and said "Cheers Mick, tha can keep that"

Brenda was, as Mick feared, the last to leave. She was in the kitchen washing the drinks glasses and tidying the work tops.

"Leave that Brenda." Said Mick. "Oyl walk you home, I need some air."

"There's no need Mick, I could stay a little longer if you wish, shall I put the kettle on?"

"No it's foin Brenda, the last thing oiy need now is more liquid, oyl be up all noight as it is."

"I could stay Mick."

"I know Brenda and thanks but…"

Brenda avoided looking at Mick and said "OK, but you know the offers there when you're ready."

Mick did the honourable thing and walked Brenda to the end of her road and accepted a kiss on his cheek as thanks.

"Shit, shit, bloody shit and shit some more, I don't think I'll ever be ready for another woman no matter how attractive they are." He thought.

Chapter 15

It never rains but it pours

"Jesus Christ, Mushy yow could ave whistled…. yow frightened the shite out of me."

"Oyl Roight Mick, I thought oyd come down and look at me new plot."

"It's the back of 'me sheds,' the raised beds. I thought they would suit you as you ain't bending so much and yow can av one of me sheds for your tools."

"Where's me spuds gooin?"

"In buckets, in bins. Don't try to kid me on, it were yow that showed me ow to grow em in containers. Yow and the missus don't need that many anymore now yow ain't feeding village and neither do I so we can share what we grow." The realisation seemed to have just dawned on Mick that he too lived in a reduced household and tons of fresh veg were no longer required and hadn't been since Josie sadly passed.

"Morning Mick, morning Mushy," interrupted Old Windy.

"Looks like we're avin an old farts convention 'ere. What's up 'Councillor' Ow long ya bin doing that?" Asked Mick.

"Has someone turned the water off, there doesn't seem to be any at the top and the hen keepers are moaning."

"Not to my knowledge mate, Mushy do you know owt, yow've got the mains key?"

"Ow do Windy. No Mick as far as I know the key is still in me shed."

As they walked to the tap 'Wot ya doing on the Parish Council?' asked Mick.

"Missus thought it might be a good idea, a couple of other lads down here are on the council too" replied 'Windy' waiting for the disparaging remarks which never came.

After trying the nearest tap Mick, Mushy and Windy walked the allotments trying each tap and confirming that the water was definitely off.

"Some buggers turned us off in the road," suggested Mushy."

"What about our own stopcock" asked Windy?

 Sure enough by the time they reached the stopcock it was apparent that there was a major leak from it. Lifting the ground cover lid wasn't necessary as it was already up and the meter, valve and pipework had been deliberately damaged and the hammer used to do the vandalism lay on the water-logged ground.

 "Who would do that, and why?" asked Windy.

"Some twats," suggested Mushy.

"Twats or twat." thought Mick.

Speaking into his mobile phone Mick said. "Allo Marty, do yow know owt about water mains and stopcocks, we've gorra problem down the 'Lockie' some chuff as teken an 'ammer to the valve and pipework"

"Tha needs to turn it off in the street, I'll bring some gear from this site and get it sorted later today. The problem we have is who did it and why? I'm telling you now… that ain't kids." Shouted Martyn from a scaffolding somewhere.

As Mick turned he saw 'Old Ben' chasing after his hens.

"I wonder if Ben saw anything." He remarked.

"Ben? Get a grip Mick he passed away ten years ago." Replied Windy.

"Oh Jesus, roight, sorry lads." Apologised Mick as he watched Old Ben running across his plot after hens that had probably been as dead as long he had been. "I lost me bearings for a while."

"And yur fuckin marbles." Chided Mushy.

Back at his plot Mick asked the others if they fancied a cup of tea. When he picked up his kettle it felt suspiciously full, he tipped it and out ran a straw coloured liquid... "Someone's pissed in me kettle.... The bastards!"

"We've only been gone a while." Noted Windy.

"Yes, I know but I don't lock me shed, no point as everything is old and knackered like me. Some twat knew that and has been playing games."

"Inside the shed and not pissing out." thought Mick. "If I catch the..."

"Ey up Mick." Interrupted Len. "As tha got five minutes?"

"Allo Len, it must be bad to bring you over from Dolethorpe, I'd offer you a drink but some bastards pissed in me kettle."

"Aye we're having problems too Mick, we need a chat."

With that both Windy and Mushy announced they would turn off the mains and then head for home leaving Mick and Len alone with the only option but to go to the 'Flying Slug.'

"Smashed Greenhouses, burgled sheds, plants trodden down and fencing damaged. It's been happening this past week. We've set up a night watch to catch the bastards and that'll probably drive the little buggers over here or Muxborough." Announced Len as they chose a table near the door and far enough away from the lunch time crowd of three.

"What makes yow think its kids?" asked Mick.

"Because it vandalism, nothing of value that could be traced has been taken, just old junk tools and then there's the plants, cabbages kicked like footballs, Chrysanths and dahlias pulled up. Adults wouldn't have left any clues that they had been nosing around and stealing"

"Ave yow heard if any other sites, apart from us, as 'ad problems? Asked Mick.

"Not that I know of Mick that's why I came. I reckon we should have a secretaries meeting without involving that pillock at Dolethorpe, he'd only use it to his advantage."

"But I'm the chairman here, Bryan Parkin is our secretary."

"If it's to be on the 'Q T' would he be any the wiser?"

"I suppose so, ar goo on then set one up and tell us when and where." replied Mick before thinking "I've bloody done it again… 'Icarus bleedin Mickarus', sorry Josie yow were right, Oim 'the mouth from the South' and oive scored another bleedin home goal.

Chapter 16

Jesus 'H' Christ

Two hours after Len had left the pub Mick decided to go home. He had no idea why he stayed so long, perhaps the prospect of an empty house was worse than having to endure the glum surrounding and banal chit chat with a mirthless landlord though he did pick up a few snippets about Sid Davies!

"About turn O'Rearden." Ordered Martyn. "We've been to your house to see you but you ain't in, so we've found ya… Get them in."

As Martyn made his way through the door he was followed by Brenda, Colin and Bryan.

"Wot's up?" asked Mick

"A Pint, a glass of Rosé, two halves of cider and a sherry for 'the newbie' parking the car and oh, get yourself one seeing as it's your round." Laughed Martyn.

'Another one?' queried 'Droopy' who then he announced, "He's had five whiskey's before you got here!"

"Five?" Exclaimed Brenda. "Why are you hitting the bottle, celebrating something?"

"More like remorse and yes gaffer, I'll have another one."

"What's up with you? Said Bryanne and Coleen in unison

"Nowt, I'm glad you're here we need to up our security after this morning's attack on the water…."

"Sorted" Martyn interjected.

"Thanks Martyn, but it may ave been just the start, Len tells me they have a night shift at Dolethorpe allotments because of the wanton damage they've had over the past couple of days. Len thinks its kids but it may be deliberate attacks."

"Bye whom?" Coleen and Brenda were in unison this time.

"Don't know." said Mick. "But there's some dodgy stuff happening under our noses. 'Arsto Homes' have been shown around Dolethorpe...."

"Ey, that's what I was on about." Interrupted Martyn. "But I din't know it was an allotment site the gaffers were on about."

"Yes mate and that's why I need you to keep sniffing around on the quiet, we all need to keep quiet about what's happening. If any of us get wind of anything or sees anything we need to share it within the committee only."

"Well, let us tell you our good news." Brenda said excitedly. "The accounts have been transferred to us.... We have the princely sum of nine hundred pounds and a bit. All our plots are now taken. Halving the larger ones has encouraged more interest, from women I might add, and Walter has applied for a lottery grant to improve disabled access which will benefit the community."

Walter added. "We can have open days, demonstrations, allotment market days, all sorts of thing which will strengthen us against Dolethorpe Council... Which Councillor is going to vote to shut a community asset? I have completed the new rules and included security, health and safety assessments, fire regulations and animal husbandry guidelines..."

"Tha Watt?" chided Martyn.

"Yes, well... By being more inclusive I think we will stymy our opponents. I am still looking into our relationship with Dolethorpe Council and if I may Michael, I'd like to see the documents Mushy' handed over."

"My turn" said Martyn. "And you deserve another sherry, in fact a 'Schooner' of sherry." He said patting an embarrassed Walter on his back.

Brenda then said "Both Colin and Bryan deserve some recognition in promoting the allotments, those flyers they posted through the door were works of art, and, they paid for the printing!"

"Alright, alright… I'll get everyone a drink"

"We didn't post one through Fatty Davis's door… he can go whistle." Colin said winking at Mick.

"Well this is all good news, oive eard in 'ere tonight that Sid has been buying drinks for any tenants he meets in here and cosying up to them. As oy said earlier we need to keep ower eyes and ears open an we all need to build on the good work yower are all dooin."

Brenda came back with the bad news… "Sorry everyone…we have been given notice of our rent increase... Dolethorpe Council have written to say our rent has been reviewed and we are to pay £592 per year...

"Tell them t'bollocks." Interrupted Marty.

"Ang fire mate, I don't think they can and I don't think wot they're askin is legal, we need sum advice, we need more info. Just keep the demand Brenda, in fact send me a copy because I want to know why it weren't sent to me."

Mick wanted to tell them all the parts of the puzzle he had discovered, or imagined because of his hatred of Sid Davies, but he knew that drink and talk had been the downfall of many managers and union men... keep your cards close to your chest... chest... chest... Jesus... Jesus fucking 'H' Christ... Darkness, deep, deep darkness!

Chapter 17

Spud Murphy

"Hello Michael, I'm Sister Holland. Welcome back. You've had a bit off a scare. How are feeling?"

"Wot appened, ow did oy get here?"

"We think you may have had a bit of a heart scare Michael, you were lucky your friends knew how to give you CPR. Doctor will be along to see you soon, just rest and don't worry too much, your awake and with us that's what matters most."

"Wot's all this gubbins?"

"You're wired to some monitors Michael, just rest easy while we do some readings, doctors will be back soon." Replied the nurse.

"Doctors, I've shit em." Thought Mick.

He closed his eyes. The searing pain had left his chest but he still felt a lot of discomfort. Back in the darkness he tried to remember what had happened. His consciousness was filled with noises from nurses and sounds of hurt and suffering. Trollies were being moved about and a child was crying.

"See to the Babby first, I'm OK." He said just as the darkness came back.

"Spud. What you doing here after all these years? Bloody ell where av yow bin?"

Spud Murphy had been his best mate for years, Mick had been Godfather to both his kids. They stood together on picket lines during the miners' strike and Mick had shared his allotment vegetables with him when the strike pay was drying up. It had been the longest miners' strike since the 1920's and a lot of families suffered because of it but a lot of lifelong bonds were made in spite of it.

Mick and Josie often gave up food so that 'Spud's' kids would have a meal. Josie used to take the children out for a treat but brought them home with new shoes or coats along with the 'McDonalds Happy Meals.' She'd often stand at the kitchen sink saying "Those poor kids, those poor, poor kids, it's not right Mick."

"What would yow ave us do Josie?" Mick asked. "Dyow want us to break the strike and be scabs like that piece of shit Davies and his mates?"

Josie knew Mick had fought for injustice as long as she had known him. He was the first one to pick up the banner before the drums started to beat. He rallied the others round when lesser men thought they were facing defeat. She often thought he should have been a politician but he was too altruistic. Politicians were and are often disingenuous and selfish by nature whereas Mick's door was always open to his neighbours and workmates regardless of whether their views conflicted with his own. He was the only Mineworkers Union official who refused to make a political contribution from his union dues. However he suffered fools lightly as Sid Davies found out when he came begging for legal support having been caught shoplifting.

"No help for thieving scabs." Mick had said when he slammed the door shut in Davies's face.

She told him perhaps he had been too harsh and that he should consider why Sid was a striker breaker. Mick reminded her of Spud Murphy and all the others who supported the strike despite having families. He told her to think about all the people in the village and the country who were going without to improve their, and Sid Davies's lives and then, surprisingly' he told her he sympathised with the strike breakers who were to be castigated for their actions in support of their families then asked how many of them had stolen and pretended to be on strike while drawing pay.

"Look at Spud Murphy." He said. "Ow d'ya think 'e feels when oym buying is beer and geeing him veg while yow're out buying clothes for is kids. 'He ain't ever been shoplifting, he ain't lying and he din't sneak off to work before anyone was up…. No, he was a decent bloke…

"Spud….what you doing here after all these years? Who the fuck is trying to kiss me?"

Through the darkness he could see Brenda leaning over him. Spud was behind her and was saying "Not now Mick, not now."

"Bloody ell Brenda, gie ower will ya, I want to see me mate Spud, stop bloody kissing me will ya, Spud what ya on about, not now?"

"Hello Mr. O'Rearden I'm doctor Khan, a cardiologist. Can you remember what happened?"

"Oy ad these terrible pains in me chest next thing me mate Spud Murphy was there and…"

"Lucky for you he was Michael… and lucky for you your friend knew what to do in an emergency. Looking at your results, I don't think you had a cardiac arrest but you are not far from having one. I believe you are suffering from CAD or coronary artery disease. It's brought on by blockage in the heart blood vessels that reduces blood flow and oxygen to the heart muscle. It's known as 'Angina'. Have you heard of 'Angina'? It's a symptom of heart disease luckily for you it doesn't cause permanent damage to the heart. It is, though, a sign that you are a candidate for a heart attack at some point in the future. Looking at your blood test results you seem to have been abusing alcohol. Is drinking a regular habit of yours, How many units do you drink a week?"

"Units?" thought Mick." Who the fuck drinks units?" "No idea Doc. The only person who checked on my drinking passed away years ago. I suppose I have been a bit heavy when pouring since then."

"Well it's taking its toll, you need to seriously cut back or maybe the next time.... I'm adding you to my appointment list and prescribing you Statins and Beta Blockers...You need to stop drinking and rest, and in the meantime I'm referring you to a drink councillor."

Mick thought. "A drink councillor...Will they prescribe some units... get fucked... Doctors. I've shit them!"

"Ey up Reardo, ow ya doing?" It was Mushy Peace. "Come tu visit ya, what's the food loik in ere? Thought yow wur a gonna there mate, I nearly had all your plot and all yur veg. By the way...Where's the shed keys?"

"Sheds not locked ya cheeky twat... How did they let a scruff like you in a hospital, what appened to Spud Murphy, he was there when I collapsed?

"For fucks sake Mick, yow really as lost thee marbles... Spud died years ago over at Wakefield... Oy thought yow ad eard seeing as ow e were ya mate. He couldn't have been there, Yow was hallucinating or summat. From what I know Marty Shyler was geeing thee a thump in the chest and Brenda, ya lucky fucker, was geein yow the kiss of life. If I'd have been there I'd ave felt your knackers so as you'd ave thought it were er."

Mick closed his eyes and thought "Spud, were at the meeting at Dolethorpe.... Fucking ell...whose next?"

Chapter 18

The Secret Secretaries Meeting

Len opened the meeting by saying, "Here's the deal Mick, we have all had increased bills from the council. We can't pay them without trebling or even quadrupling rents… tenants ain't gonna pay…so we'll have empty plots and no money coming in to pay the council so we'll be in default."

"On top of all that we are all getting damage and trespass, so tenants are having to pay for repairs and replacements, they won't be too happy with a rent increase, they'll just pack in." Added Gordon Jones.

"Mark toime lads, we've ad bills, we ain't ad demands or threats yet. It's that pillock Russel flexing 'is muscles."

The meeting, as Len had promised, was a collective of allotment secretaries from sites that came under the auspices of Dolethorpe Council. Sites that had all seen increases and some that had also seen Arsto vans in or near their sites.

"Old on a minute, who elected me as chairman? I came along in support, I'm not even a secretary!'

"Mick you have a lot of respect in this borough and a lot of lads know you as the best union rep we had, you ain't thick like the rest of us and you'll take them on just to give them a bloody nose so they know we ain't taking this lying down." Contributed a bloke who Mick had never seen before but who obviously held him in high esteem.

"That's all well 'n gud but me foightin days ar over"

"We know you ain't been well lately Mick, but perhaps you could see your way to advise us on how we are going to take them on"

"Dear God, 'Icarus Bleeding Mickarus'" thought Mick.

After asking for their percentage rent increases Mick agreed to give it some thought and said would look into any shortcoming he could see. Len said he would be the group's secretary or 'conduit' so no one knew what they were doing and asked for all thoughts and ideas to be sent to him first and he asked for secrecy.

When 'Icarus Bleeding Mickarus' arrived home he opened a whisky bottle without any consideration to his health. "Been there, done that." he thought as he poured the first large drink of the evening.

Staring at a blank TV … "best programmes are when it's switched off." He thought. "Mind you that gardening presenter with the big knockers… 'And dirty broken finger nails' as Josie reminded him every time she was on, managed to keep his attention but then he never saw her hands!

Brenda had said the rents for Frighall allotments had gone to £592 a year from £12 a year that's a bloody big jump he thought while trying to work out the percentage increase. He was hopeless at maths so every time he tried he got a different figure even the calculator he found in the kitchen draw didn't give a right sounding result. 'Batteries must be knackered." He said to himself as he went to the phone. He knew he should phone Brenda about financial matters but…

"Hello Walter"

"Hello Mick, how are you, are the tablets working?"

"Oim foin mate but I think the tablets are robbin me brain, I can't for the loif ov me remember how to do percentage increases…"

"Nearly five thousand percent Mick if you trying to work out our rent increase. I couldn't believe it when Brenda told us, I did the sums when I got home."

"That can't roight. It must be illegal or summat. I need to gie this some real thought. Thanks for listening to me and elping Oy'l come back" With that Mick hung the call up on a bewildered Walter.

Sat back in front of the blank TV screen he pondered over the union battles he'd had with the gaffers and he poured another drink... the good angel on his right shoulder tutted while the devil on his left said "Doctors, you've shit them."

"Equality, equality." He thought "We ain't all been charged the same!" Albeit the sites were different in acreage the percentage increases he noted at the meeting were all different.

"Walter, it's me again, sorry mate, Oi've ad a light bulb moment. Can yow get on yur computer and find out what the council rent increases are for all the departments are in Dolethorpe, Oi've ad an idea."

Walter agreed to come back after he had done some checking.

"When the Coal Board wanted more coal all pits were given the same target because it was obvious that the larger sites would produce more coal for the same percentage increase so why are allotments getting different rent demands when it should be fixed across the borough." Thought Mick. "I would have took the pit gaffers to a tribunal in the old days if they had tried the same trick as old Brussel Sprout thinks he's gonna get away with."

After an hour Walter phoned with the news that most of the services had a ten percent increase for the current financial year. "They had trouble getting that passed the councillors according to the minutes and get this... the Gardens and Recreation department were fixed at six percent because they had charged more in previous years and had objected." Reported Walter.

"Good lad, we need an urgent committee meeting ere tomorrow night, Can yow mek it?"

"Certainly, I'll ring around the others, what's your plan Mick or is it too soon?"

"Oyl let ya now tomorrow, tell them six thirty ere will ya and thanks."

A phone call to Len inviting him over to his committee meeting confirmed he had already decided his next step. "We'll need another secret secretaries meeting Len, and soon Oy'll call ya again tomorrow with sum facts but keep shtum will ya."

Chapter 19

Emergency Meeting

After introducing Len, Mick, told the committee he wanted some quick action to take place on the plots.

"We need rubbish skips to get shut of all the chemicals, paints, weed killers and junk in people's sheds. All plots need to be checked against Walter's Health and Safety guidelines. Marty can yow start that as soon as pos. Windy, can yow and Mushy check on the hen keepers, their runs need to be spotless with no signs of vermin. Tell them we're worried about reports of 'Bird Flue' and need to reduce the risk of contamination. Any problems or arguments, tell them it's because we are part of Dolethorpe Council now."

"Len, can yow do the same at your site and ask the other sites in the borough to do the same, yow know them better than me."

"Walter, can yow share our new rules and guides with Len so he can update theirs."

"What's happening Mick and why does Len need to share with the other sites?" Asked a concerned Brenda.

"Oym drawing up sum battle lines Brenda, we need to be prepared for a fight wi the council. They ave notified yow ov a five thousand percent increase so oym gonna fight em. If they walk away from us they'll only pick on another site so everyone needs to be ready."

"Colin and Brian, we need a tenants meeting as soon as possible because we need them all to sign the new tenants agreement quickly. Can yow get everyone there. If they can't come, get em to sign the agreement when they give their excuses."

"Fatty Sid Davis won't agree." Said Colleen.

"Oive a feeling he'll only be too glad to sign." Replied Mick.

Len had already been briefed earlier of Mick's intentions and although unfair not to fully brief his committee he never the less did tell them that earlier he had consulted with the firm of Harrison and Harrison solicitors who had agreed to act on his behalf as an individual in his fight against Dolethorpe Council. He had decided to take the fight on not as a society, but in his own name because if it went 'tits up' he'd be the one who was kicked off his plot though he absolutely certain they couldn't even do that.

Earlier Mick had also spoken to Tracy at Russell's office and asked her if she could send him copies of all communications between Dolethorpe and the Frighall Allotments and Garden Society. "Sorry I can't." She had replied. "Ave yow bin told not too?" Asked Mick. "Because Oy could request em under the Freedom Ov Information Act." He had used it once before and created absolute chaos at Frighall Colliery with the same request and almost shut the HR department down while all the staff searched for the information he had requested.

"No it's not that Mr O'Rearden, it's because we don't seem to have any copies of any letters other than the ones asking Mr. Peace to come to the meeting with Mr Russell and one from Finance informing your society of the rent increase. After the meeting, I was asked to put a file together and to be quite honest, that's all that's in the file!"

So the only information they had was less than what he had in Mushy's briefcase. "Got em." He thought. "Thanks Tracy, you're a star."

Having served everyone with refreshments Mick looked around the room at the faces looking back at him in bewilderment.

"Look Oim doin this on me own back, yow ain't got now't to worry about... All I want is yower support when the shit it's the fan, if it gus wrong then yow've got nowt tu worry about. If it, as I suspect, cums out smelling ov roses, yow'll owe me a pint.

Marty asked "Is Sid Davis mine? I'd love to march him off the site on behalf of all the blokes he's shit on."

"Not yet mate, we need to go softlee, softlee catchee monkee."

"Mick if you are going to take the council on our behalf... you need to cut back on the booze, you had three large ones while we've been here. I thought the doctor told you to slow down." Suggested Brenda.

"Thanks Brenda, but this is a foight and I am up for it. Oim am eternally grateful to yow and Marty, but this is me foight and oi've sum old scores to settle."

The following evening the 'Secret Secretaries' met and Mick told them that for their own sakes he wasn't going to tell them the full facts and he outlined only what he had told his own committee. He asked them for support in updating all their rules and in cleaning up their sites so that they couldn't be found wanting if Russell wanted do inspections.

He did tell them however that he thought the recent vandalism was deliberate and was meant to scare tenants off so plots lay vacant with no rent coming in to their societies and associations. He suggested that vacant plots should be let rent free for the first year and recommended that they do as Brenda had suggested and halve some of the plots so they were more easily manageable by those with other commitments and his used his site as an example of having all the plots filled in a couple of weeks.

He told them to raise their profiles in their communities so that if problems arose with the council they would have local support.

"You do know the council is obliged in law to provide residents with allotments." Suggested Harry Hibbert the secretary for Deanby.

"Yes." replied Mick. "An Dolethorpe can say they're complying with the law by aving one site a bus ride away and that site will be full and have a very long waiting list. All Oim asking for is yower support and secrecy while oim fightin them. Yow need to act quickly because they may concede to me and then attack you. 'Arsto' are wantin to build ouses round ere and the council need the money so put two and two together we're soft targets at the moment."

"Oh, another thing, try not to tell anyone why as yow'll blow me cover, we'll all lose an oyl be fucking angry we whoever talks."

Chapter 20

Gardener's 'Questionable' Time

"Mick." shouted Brenda. "Some policemen are coming down the barrow path."

Mick looked up from weeding and saw Al Symer pointing in his direction. The policemen carried on down the barrow path followed, as expected, by a couple of tenants that had long since given up any worries about rent arrears.

"Wonder what they want?" She added.

"They look like they want to press their trousers and polish their shoes." Thought Mick.

"Mr. O'Rearden?" Asked the smaller of the two. Before Mick had confirmed his name the other said. "We need to ask you some questions about damage to allotment property"

"Can you tell us where you were yesterday evening?"

"Ar The day before I had a meeting wi ower committee at my ouse then as a result last night I went to a meeting with other allotment secretaries, why?"

"Where was that meeting, what time was it held and what time did it finish?"

"Adick Road Allotments committee hut, 7 until 8... Check the minutes. We discussed damage to property on allotments across the Borough. Why do yow lot want t'know any ow?"

"We have had a complaint about you and we're here to ask you to come to Dolethorpe Police station to answer some further questions and to make a statement in relation to the complaint. You can come along with us or make your own way there but we need to talk to you today"

"Gie me an 'our, oyl come to yow when Oive ad a wash n shave." Mick replied and then thought. "A complaint about me.... I wonder who from, as if I didn't know!"

As the cops walked back up the barrow path they were being escorted off site by the 'dearly departed' who had been joined by several more all of whom were surrounding the officers and giving them the single finger or the V sign. "Yow wouldn't ave done that to proper coppers." Thought Mick as Brenda approached.

"What was that about Mick?" She asked.

"Just elping with their enquiries, oi've to go to the cop shop... will fill ya in later but it's about the damage that's bin appening."

Entering the portals of Dolethorpe police station wasn't new to Mick. He had been in many times to plead for striking miners whose aggressiveness had upset 'wet behind the ear' coppers who had never had to fight for their rights or the right to feed their kids.

"Hello Mr. O' Rearden, thanks for coming in I am Detective Sergeant Hurst, I understand that my colleagues have told you why you have been asked to come in today."

"Oiv bin told it's about a complaint against me, must be serious if a Detective Sergeant is handling it, what's the complaint and who made it?"

"The complaint is that you are responsible for damage which occurred on Adick Road Allotments. I understand you admitted to officers that you were there yesterday evening."

Mick looked at the policeman and saw that he was probably ready for retirement and had picked himself an easy job. "I don't know much about the law but isn't this an allegation not a complaint. Who made the allegation? "Asked Mick

"No you don't know much about the law." Replied Hurst. "An allegation is a statement of factual matter, at the moment I am regarding the matter as a complaint until my questioning shows any difference. What I do know is that you have already admitted to being at Adick Road and that damage occurred to property there. Now that may just be coincidental but the complainant has said that you caused the damage and that you may be responsible for damage occurring on other sites."

"So the complainant is mekin allegations!" laughed Mick. "Who is it so we can find out what their grievance with me is? For God sake man, I was in the company of the bloody Adick Road Secretary and a lot other secretaries too, we met to discuss the bloody damage I am 'Alleged' to have carried out."

"Do you recognise this Mr. O'Rearden?" Asked the officer as he opened his desk drawer.

"Yes it me pit deputies yardstick, ow have yow got it? Should be in me shed, has bin for years, I use it for measure me rows and planting out. Yow can see the marking and if yow turn it yowl see me name and me pit number. Ow ave yow gorrit?" Mick asked angrily.

"It was found amongst the glass in a smashed greenhouse this morning, now shall we continue with my questions.... how did it get there O'Rearden, Did you take it to the meeting, did you stay behind to do the damage, why would you want to do that?" Smirked the officer who felt he had Mick over a barrel.

"Oy left the bloody site wi the secretary who locked the gate after we ad all left, do yow think oim that stupid that I'd do damage to greenhouses the same bloody night oy was there with witnesses? Oyl tell ya where to direct ya questions shall oy, at the fat shit that's med this up and oy suggest yow tell im to come and av a cup of tea in my shed only this toime oyl piss in the kettle. Oim done ere Detective Sergeant so unless yow ar gonna arrest me oim off.

Mick got up to walk away. "I haven't finished my questions O' Rearden... sit down." demanded Hurst.

"Here's summat for yow to ponder" Replied Mick "We were avin a secret meeting. Nobody outside the group of secretaries knew about it, yow asked if it was a coincidence... "Yes it was a co-incidence" It was a coincidence that the thick pillock who as been going around ruining the people's obbies picked the rung site on the rung night... That yardstick could ave bin teken from me unlocked shed at any toime. Ask yourself ow I know its Sid Davis making the complaint, ask that dodgy fucker some more questions before yow decide whether it's an allegation or a complaint, ask him for his alibis for all the nights damage as occurred and when yow've finished oyl ave me yardstick back."

Mick arrived home and had barely time to put the kettle on or pour drink when the phone rang... so he poured a drink while he was talking.

"Brenda Luv, yow wouldn't believe it. They are only trying to blame me for all the damage that's happening on all the sites." Was Micks reply to Brenda. "They even ad me yardstick as evidence, it was found in a smashed up greenhouse at Adick Road. And because I was there last night I'm chief suspect, yow couldn't mek it up. I left them with a flea in their ears and some questions they need answering before they talk to me again."

"Well that's ridiculous Mick, for a start you were in hospital the night Deanby site had damage. You need to sit down and think where you have been on the evenings things were damaged and if you haven't got an alibi I'll say you were with me. Don't get upset and stressed about it, remember what the doctor has said."

"That's probably the only night I have got an alibi, I'm on me lonesome nearly every night" He thought then said. "Thanks Brenda but I don't think it will come to anything, they'll end up blaming kids to save themselves some paperwork." Before he realised what he was saying he had asked her if she fancied going for a meal by way of thanks for saving his life. When she said yes he thought. "Bugger, bollocks and double bollocks. Icarus Bleeding Mickarus, Tha's done it again."

Chapter 21

The Postman knocks twice.

Dear Mr. O' Rearden

Ref: 12-568/16b - O'Rearden versus Dolethorpe Council

In accordance with your instructions we have served notice of your rent appeal upon Dolethorpe Council. To date we still await their response, although this is usually normal when dealing with local authorities, we did expect a quick response given that the authority is due to set its budget for the forthcoming year.

Recognising that there may be implications for other allotment societies and associations we have written to the Royal Association for Allotments and Gardens outlining the steps you have taken and requesting that they share any similar experiences that they may have.

RAAG have very kindly replied but declined to share information as they state your society is no longer a member of the National Association. We have clarified with them, by phone, that you are acting alone, that you are not seeking financial assistance from them and that you only wish to see parity across all local authorities to the benefit of all societies and gardeners.

Further investigations have shown that RAAG have been, since 1921, in receipt of grants from several authorities. In our opinion this fact alone would be a deterrent for them to assisting in any action against their benefactors and may be an indicator of the opposition you may face in any legal proceedings that may pursue from your appeal. It is of our opinion that because of their reliance on grants, RAAG are more likely to support the landlords and not the tenants.

Given the need, on their part, for expediency we expect to hear from them very soon. In the interim we would ask you to share, as soon as possible, any communications you may have with them and we would ask that you confirm that you are prepared, given the stance of the National Association, to continue in what may be an expensive action.

Yours Sincerely

"Too fuckin roight oy wish to continue… never backed away from a foight we gaffers yet, fuck RAAG too, they did jack shit for the money we give them, once a year send out 2 copies of their shite magazine for 50 tenants which tells us ow they are swanning of around Europe visiting other National Associations. Fucking jobs for the boys, well they can bollocks too." Mick said aloud to an empty kitchen where stood checking his mail.

Our ref: BR 1212

Dear Chairman

Re: Frighall Allotments and Gardens Society

We are in receipt of a rent appeal in respect of our notice to you that your allotment society's rent is to increase for the forth-coming financial year.

Having given the matter our consideration we are conscious that increases of this amount may cause immediate difficulties for small societies such as yours and as such would like to offer your group time to pay.

Our Finance Department can set up four quarterly staged payments which we believe may be helpful and reduce your burden of finding the money. We are aware that our demand has come before you are able to warn your tenants of the potential rent increase and how it may affect them individually.

Taking advantage of the staged payment offer does not incur interest charges but does require your society to sign a new contract with the authority.

"New contract be fucked, Yow ain't got an old contract!"

Should you wish to take up the offer of staged payments we would ask that you contact 'The Allotment Officer' as soon as possible and that signed copies of the new contract are returned to him forthwith.

Failure to do so would render your society in default of our agreement if full payment is not made by the due date in our notice of your rent increase.

Yours Faithfully…

"Our agreement? We ain't got an agreement, we ain't got a contract so yow can bollocks."

The whiskey bottle was out and Mick was pacing the kitchen. "Dear Chairman… Dear Chairman. Neither the fucking chairman nor the fucking society have raised an appeal… oy ave me Mick O'Rearden when are yow writing to me? No fucking wonder Mushy binned yur letters."

It was clear that faced with a challenge their tactics had changed now they were trying to trick him into signing a contract where the allotment society would be at the mercy of Russel and he would have inadvertently accepted the very rent increase he had appealed against.

"Our ref: BR 1212. That's his fucking telephone number and his initials. As Tracy gie me a clue when she typed it up… is 'e working of his own back, well yow ave met yower match 'Sprouty' old boy, yow ave met yower match."

Knowing he couldn't drive because he'd had a drink, or two, while reading the letters Mick phoned Len and told him he would meet him in the 'The Rusty Dudley' after he had called into Harrisons the solicitors. The walk into Dolethorpe wasn't long and he was hoping it would give him chance to clear his head and decide how he was going to win this battle but the more he thought of Russel the angrier he got and the angrier he got the faster he walked and the faster he walked greater the pressure he felt on his chest.

Taking five minutes rest at a bus stop he realised 'Spud Murphy' was stood beside him.

"Wot appened to yow" He asked. "No fucker told me yow ad passed"

He watched as Spud held a finger to his lips and say "Not now, Not now" and then he was gone again.

As he entered the 'Rusty Dudley' Sid Davies barged passed him and left the pub. Len waved and called him to the table he was at.

"Just had an interesting conversation with your mate. How does he know you have appealed the rent increase, I thought it was a secret."

"It is, Oive just teken some letters to the solicitors... Some twat is briefing him and oy thinks its Brussel Sprout.

After outlining the story of the morning post he said "We need to tell all the secretaries and treasurers not to agree to any staged payments to ease the increases. It's a back door way to sign up to new agreements at the very least they'll more than likely ave a termination clause in them that no fucker can meet, Tell em all to lodge an objection against the increase, they don't need a solicitor, just a letter to delay them until my appeal as bin eard"

Mick had barely arrived home when the postman knocked. "Sorry Mick, you were out when I came earlier. I need a signature for this one mate."

"Thanks Mucker, I was probably down the allotment or in the back garden, what's this un about?"

"Looking at the envelope Mick it ain't good, delivered a few of them during the strike, it could be a court summons."

Dolethorpe Magistrate Courts
Court Hearing Scheduled
Name: Michael O' Rearden

You are hereby summoned to appear on **Friday 13ᵗʰ September at 2.00 pm** before the Magistrates Court High Street Dolethorpe to answer the following;

That you Michel O' Rearden are alleged to have committed the offences listed here:

Criminal Damage to property at *The Allotments Britannia Road Dolethorpe.*

Criminal Damage to property at *The Allotments Adick Road Muxborough.*

Criminal Damage to property at *The Allotments Church Lane Deanby.*

Criminal Damage to property at *The Allotments Manvers Road Dolethorpe*

You **must** attend the Magistrates Court at the time and date stated to answer the charges.

Dolethorpe Magistrates Court Friday 13ᵗʰ September 2.00pm

If you do not attend, the court may hear the case in your absence and may issue a warrant for your arrest. If a warrant is issued for your arrest, you may be held in custody until you are brought before the court.

The full explanation of the offences is shown overleaf.

"Well ain't that dandy, looks like yow've got another fight on 'Icarus Bleeding Mickarus' Poor old Josie would be turning in er grave if she knew I was teking the council and the cops on!"

Thinking of Josie reminded him of his offer to Brenda and he began to regret it even more so. He phoned her and after a chat about the latest letter he asked could they delay the meal until after the court case. She reluctantly agreed and even offered to cook a meal for him at her house which he in turn 'reluctantly' refused making up some codswallop about not wanting any distractions. "Phew, got out of that one." He thought. "But for how long?"

Chapter 22

Dolethorpe Magistrates Court

"Well Mr. O'Rearden it would seem that the police, in their wisdom, have obviously decided that the alleged crimes are of a minor nature otherwise known 'Summary Offences' these are are smaller crimes that can be punished under the magistrates' courts limited sentencing powers... You do not have the option of trial by jury. However, I must warn you that magistrates have the power to refer you to a Crown Court where more severe punishments may be handed out. We need to ensure that you are able to provide an alibi for your whereabouts on each of the dates."

"Sorry Mr. Harrison but Oy can't, I live alone and with the exception of one date Oive no alibis. The damage to the allotments at Deanby is supposed to av occurred oy was in hospital, oy was kept in overnight for observations."

"Did you explain this to the police officer who questioned you?"

"Oy didn't get the chance, I didn't know what or where I was supposed to have been until that letter came through the door."

"Well we can stop this immediately by calling the officer and asking him to verify his witnesses statement, clearly their witness has been fabricating some or all of the facts."

"No, Oy want me day in court, I want the press there too. I want Mr. Sidney Arthur Davies to be seen to have been wasting police time again and I want him to say who put him up to it because Oy think there's a bit of jiggery pokery going on. So Oy'll be glad if yow represent me on this case too."

On the date of the hearing the courts were unusually full and it would seem there was a lot of interest in this hearing.

Mick was met at the court by his solicitor Harrison Jnr. "Well Mick, a reporter from the Yorkshire Clarion is here and so are some of your allotment friends, they have asked me to pass on their best wishes. We should go in." Once in the court room he then explained that the chap in the black gown was an 'Usher' and that he was only there to administer on behalf of the magistrates In front of the 'Bench' sat a legal advisor whose job was ensure that the magistrates handed out the correct sentence or followed the correct procedures. He then pointed out the prosecution solicitor 'Mr Tucker' whose role he said "Is to convince everyone that you are guilty."

Sat in front of Tucker was Detective Sergeant Hurst and Sid Davis who seemed to have borrowed a suit, washed his face and had his haircut for the occasion.

A quick glance around the room showed that the committee had turned up in support as had the officials from all the local allotment sites. Sat at the back trying to make himself as inconspicuous as possible was none other than Bernard Russel.

"Fuck You." Thought Mick.

"All Rise." Called the usher. The magistrates came into the room and took up their seats.

Mick was asked to confirm his name and address and was then asked how he pleaded after each of the offences were read out.

"Not Guilty." Was repeated four times.

For the prosecution Tucker then started to explain to the magistrates what the allegations were.

"Your Worships, may we start with the case against my client relating to the alleged offence said to have occurred at Deanby Allotments?" Asked Harrison.

"Your Worships I intend to show that the damage occurred at the sites followed a pattern which would prove that the defendant had a motive for causing the damage."

"Proceed with the prosecution in the order of the summons. Mr. Harrison you will get your chance when you make the case for the defence."

"Thank you... Mr O'Rearden can explain where you were the night damage occurred at Britannia Road allotments"

"At Home"

"Do you have any witnesses to that effect?"

"No. do yow have any witnesses that I was in Dolethorpe?"

"All in good time Mr. O'Rearden, all in good time, do you recognise this? He asked holding up the yardstick.

"Yes, it's mine and was kept in my unlocked shed"

"Can you explain why it was found amongst the damage at Britannia Road Allotments?"

"Can yow explain ow the police said it was found at Adick Road?"

Harrison stood up. "Your Worships can you direct my honourable friend to explain why this piece of evidence has changed from Adick Road to Britannia Road. My client was shown this when questioned over the alleged offence at Adick Road"

"Your Worships Detective Sergeant Hurst offers the court and the defendant his sincere apologies in that when collating the evidence for prosecution a junior police officer had wrongly labelled the item."

Harrison stood again. "Your Worships, surely this renders the item as inadmissible evidence and my honourable friend must know that. My client was questioned about another offence and shown the item as evidence of his presence there. He has not been questioned about any other offences."

The legal advisor was on his feet whispering to the magistrates who then ordered that the yardstick had become inadmissible as evidence and ordered the prosecution to bring forward any other evidence or witnesses.

"Please confirm your name."

"Sidney Davis"

"Please read from the card." Instructed the usher.

"I do solemnly, sincerely and truly declare and affirm that the evidence I shall give shall be the truth the whole truth and nothing but the truth."

"Mr. Davis will you explain to the court what you saw or heard on Britannia Road Dolethorpe."

"Well I was walking home from my sisters, she lives at the top end of the road, as I passed the allotments I heard the sound of glass breaking, and I thought it might be kids doing some damage, so I stepped in closer to the hedge, sort off hiding like, in the hope of spotting them when they came out, I was intending to tell the families what they'd been up to but it weren't kids that come out it was him… O'Rearden. He didn't see me because he never turned around, just got in his car and drove off."

"Was Mr. O'Rearden carrying anything?"

Harrison was on his feet. "Your Worships, It has already been decided that the item has been declared inadmissible." He pleaded.

"You are correct but it has not been referred to in the question, please answer Mr. Davis."

"I don't know, I couldn't see anything as it was dark and he had his back to me."

Tucker commented. "So he may have had something under his jacket, something that he had concealed. What did you do later Mr. Davis? Did you approach the defendant?"

"When I heard about the damage I was going to, but I'm scared of him he used to bully me when we were at the pit, he was always threatening me with violence, he's a bad un. A couple of days later I was driving through Muxborough in the evening when I saw his car on Adick Road, He pulled up outside the allotments so I pulled over and watched him in my mirror. I waited about an hour when he came out with some others, but they went home and he went back in then I heard some more glass breaking….."

"Who are you pointing at, ow come you're here, I thought you were dead, why's he here too he supposed to have died years ago, It wasn't me… Why are you pointing at me…Where have you lot come from? Where's his face…Stop pointing!"

"Is there a problem Mr. Davis?" asked one of the magistrates.

"Stop pointing at me. I didn't do it!"

Both solicitors, the magistrates and everyone in the silent court room looked at Davis.

Mick clearly saw what was happening the witnesses for the defence had just arrived. They were 'Late' in more than one sense.

Davis shouted, "I ain't stopping 'ere with them, they're all dead." With that he turned and ran for the door.

"Mr. Davis, Mr. Davis." shouted the usher and Tucker but there was no stopping Davis he was off and running.

On his feet in a flash Harrison made the plea, "Your Worships the witness for the prosecution is clearly delusional, he is seeing people or things that none of us in this room can see, how can he be considered a reliable witness if he sees things that aren't here, or there? I asked that the proceedings started with the Deanby offence because my client was held in hospital on the night the damage was alleged to have occurred."

The Legal Advisor requested that the magistrates left the room to discuss what they had all witnessed.

Mick looked around the court room and saw only his friends smiling and giving thumbs up signs. Marty Shyler looked fit to burst out laughing.

"I think the case will quite rightly be thrown out Mick and I think some questions will have to be answered." Said Harrison.

"All Rise" Called the usher as the magistrates came back in.

The senior magistrate addressed the court.

"What we have seen today has been unusual to say the least however… Detective Sergeant Hurst the court will be writing to the Chief Constable asking for an explanation into how the case for the prosecution was put together, there have been far too many errors in the case not least your witness, the unfortunate Mr. Davis, who in the courts opinion is in need of psychiatric help. Added to the inadmissible evidence and your failure to question the defendant about his whereabouts on the night of the alleged offence at Deanby allotments it is of the court's opinion that this case should not have been brought before us. Mr. O'Rearden we are of the opinion that you have not committed any offence based on the evidence we have heard today. You are absolved of all the allegations and the court wishes to apologise to you for the stress and inconvenience you have suffered."

"All Rise"

"Bloody right" shouted Marty from the gallery. "Now can I have Davis?"

Mick shook Harrison's outstretched hand and walked through the door onto the street. Where he was met with cheers and cries of 'Well Done Mick' it seemed like everyone wanted to pat him on the back or shake his hand.

As he looked around he saw, across the road, Spud Murphy and several other spectres. Spud stepped forward, stood to attention and saluted while around him his ethereal companions clapped in silence. Finally Spud waved goodbye with that they all waved and disappeared.

Mick was waving back when Len asked, "What's the matter?"

"I thought I saw someone, I just feel so bloody tired, I ain't been sleeping roight lately, and Oy'll be OK after we've all had a drink… on me"

As they moved off towards the pub Russel approached him and said "You may have won a battle O'Rearden, but the wars not over"

"Did yow ear im? Mick asked the person nearest him who waved a tape recorder and nodded.

"Are yow the reporter from the 'Clarion' Yow need to do a bit of investigation into im, Davis, the bent copper and their involvement with 'Arsto Homes' all this as been set up on a purpose. Yow needs to ask why damage as only occurred on the plots that are prime building land, Yow'll ave a scoop mate."

"Yes I am, I'm Jamie Upton…can we talk Mr. O'Rearden?" He asked.

"Come to the pub we us, everyone talks after a few beers."

Driven home by Brenda Mick narrowly escaped another encounter with her by saying he needed to go to the toilet urgently. "I can come in Mick." She offered.

"Tomorrow 'Luv', tomorrow." He replied and rushed to his door. "Got out of that." He thought, "She's a lovely lass but she'll never replace yow Josie, never in a month of Sundays."

Mick sat on the edge of his bed and said to the empty room, "Well Josie, one down and one to go… 'Icarus Bleeding Mickarus' was the last thing he heard her say as he fell backwards and into a deep sleep.

Chapter 23

A sad day for Frighall

He was awakened by something tapping. "What the fuck?" he thought as he lay on the bed still fully dressed and looking at the ceiling. He looked towards the window where he could see the end of the washing line prop tapping on the window pane. Then he heard, "Mick, Mick, can you hear me? It's Tommy."

"What's up Tom? What time is it? Jeez Oive not slept like that since I was a bairn."

"Mick, I need to come in." Downstairs Mick let him in.

"What the fuck's up?"

"Bad news, I'm afraid mate, you need to sit down. I've just been to the paper shop to get a copy of the 'Clarion'… yesterday's story is all over the front page. But I ain't here for that. I've just heard that Peter Peace passed away last night."

"Who"

"Thee mate, Mushy"…

"How? When?"

"They were saying down the paper shop that after you all been to the pub he went home and was telling Beryl the story about Sid Davis and his ghosts, the one that's here in the 'Clarion'… his face is all over it… he had to sit down because he was laughing that much. Beryl went to make him a cup of tea and when she came back into the room he'd gone… Sorry Mick, but I thought you'd better know."

"Bloody ell Tom, oi've known im for most of me adult life, what the fuck, poor old Mushy… I just can't tek it in… Poor old Beryl, Oy'll ave to go and see er,"

When Tom had left he sat on the settee looking at the blank TV reminiscing all the scrapes that they had got into. He could hear

Mushy saying "Goo on oy dare ya" which was a signal for him to step in and say "yur tekin me on an all." He had my back, I had his" he thought. "He was like a big brother or me dad, e was me mate… It's shit growing old."

Stood in the shower he knew the tears weren't caused by the shampoo in his eyes, it was the heaviness in his heart, a heaviness he hadn't felt since Josie left him.

When he later called to see Beryl she had her sons and daughter with her. They still called him 'Uncle Mick' even though he was no relation and they were in their forties. No amount of expressions of grief would placate her now but she had the comfort of her family with her. He left after promising support should they need it and made sure Beryl had his phone number, "any toime day or night Beryl luv call me if yow need help or a chat." He was as upset as they were and knew the sorrow they were going through, he also knew time isn't the great healer it supposed to be when you lose someone you really love. It's definitely shit growing old.

The next few days all people he met had one comment. 'The village has lost a character.'

Chapter 24

The fight goes on

Being on the allotment gave him some solace. It was quiet and there was always something to occupy his mind although losing a close friend after agreeing to share his plot with him was in the forefront of most things he did as he tidied and cleared his beds ready for the winter. He considered giving it all up now he had little need for the veg and flowers but what else could he do? He wasn't going to sit and watch telly all day, if he went to the pub he'd only drink more than he did now and that was too much if he listened to the doctors, nurses and friends. He decided that as he had already allowed Mushy to have half the plot that it may as well be let to someone new. The thought of mentoring a new gardener pleased him and filled him with dread at the same time but his mind was made up half the plot was going.

When she was on her plot, Brenda didn't make any overt approaches as she could see Mick had quietened down since Mushy's funeral and thought perhaps he was coming to terms with his own mortality. 'A way to a man's heart is through his stomach' so today she brought him some little snacks to eat while he drank his cup of 'sergeant majors' tea and invited him for dinner at her house telling him he was under no obligation and the company would be nice for them both.

"Soon Brenda… Soon"

His mind was made up. Back home, he phoned Colleen and told him to let the back half of his plot. He then phoned Harrisons to ask them if they would make his will out and be executors as he had no family.

"I'm glad you phoned Mr. O'Rearden. There has been a development in your appeal to Dolethorpe Council. Having read their letter, which you should have been copied into, I think it's time we considered appointing a barrister. Perhaps you could pop round and will decide which way forward you want to take. Can you make it for 10am tomorrow?" asked Harrison Jnr"

"Should have been copied into… but not, them fuckers are deliberately winding me up, I should go round and rip that little toe rags fucking head off.. The wars not over 'Sprouty' but it's about to get bloody."

"Look, oive got some money, the one thing yow Yorkshire folk ave taught me is not to spend. Oy still av some of me redundancy left, there's money from Josie's insurance policy which oy ain't touched and me ouse is worth a few bob. They can all be considered for legal costs including yorn. Owt left I'll tell ya when ya write me will."

"Well, let me warn you the letter we have received has come from solicitors acting on behalf of the Local Government Association. Dolethorpe have gone large on this appeal and have the backing of the LGA because of the national implications." Replied Harrison

"Pardon my French, but fuck em, I want a barrister and I want a gud un, them twats at Dolethorpe need to learn they ain't walking over the little people anymore."

On his way home he called into an estate agents and asked them to come and value his house. He thought it might be wise given that he had just thrown it into the ring for legal costs though God knows where he'd go if he lost everything. "Sheds warm enough" he chuckled to himself.

A week later he called into the platform bar at Sheffield railway station. He was on his way to barrister's chambers and decided to bolster his courage before meeting Harrison on St. James Row. He'd looked on the map and could only see one pub near there and that was on a road called Campo Lane. Bet that's full of 'campo's' he had thought.

Two drinks later and walking to the offices he thought "Who builds a city on a bloody great hill?" He was getting breathless and wished he'd jumped into a cab as his chest was pounding and getting tighter. "Was it the angina, the exercise, the stress or the drink." he wondered?

They were ushered straight into the barrister's office where a pin stripe suit stood to meet them…It was being worn by a young woman!

"Thank you for coming along today Mr. O'Rearden, Mr. Harrison. I'm Janet Morgan. Please be seated, coffee will be here soon. You look surprised Mr. O'Rearden."

"Too tell the truth love, er sorry Miss… I always thought Barristers were crusty old men"

"Most are Mr. O'Rearden and I'll take it as a compliment. When your case was offered to these chambers I asked if I could represent you as I have specialised in Local Government law. I have read through the documents that you supplied Mr Harrison and I believe you have a very good case and that there may be implications for other allotment societies and associations. Did you know that there are over three hundred thousand allotment plots in the UK? That's a lot of people who may have been treated unfairly. To be honest I see it as a challenge and so does the Local Government Association because the implications to them will be reduced fees and possibly a refund to a lot of gardeners like yourself."

"Oim beginning to think my compliment wasn't high enough."

"Thank you again. I'm sure Mr. Harrison has explained that the process may be expensive and will most likely be dealt with by 'Judicial Review'. A judge, or judges, will be asked to review the lawfulness of a decision or action made by a public body, In other words, judicial reviews are a challenge to the way in which a decision has been made, rather than the rights and wrongs of the conclusion reached."

"So we have to prove Dolethorpe made an illegal decision to raise our rents by nearly five thousand percent" Asked Mick.

"In a nutshell" Mr. O'Rearden." My clerks have prepared 'Freedom of Information' requests to every local authority asking for specific information on allotment rental charges and increases in the last five years site by site."

"How long will it take to get this review?"

"We have to make an application to the High Court first. It can then take three to four months unless either side asks for an urgent review. Given the financial implications for Local Governments I suspect they will. You will be pleased to know that RAAG has agreed to cooperate with these chambers and will be making an application to their board to meet the costs arising from the review. I suspect they can see that a lot of their members could cancel subscriptions if they are found wanting. However it is my intention to see that the LGA are awarded all costs."

"You'll do for me darling." Thought Mick.

"You will know that Mr. Harrison has given me your instructions, if anything does not go as I plan, Mr. Harrison good offices will meet my costs and you will be indebted to him... Are happy to proceed Mr. O'Rearden?"

Minutes later they were back in the street and he had accepted a lift back to Dolethorpe from Harrison.

"She seemed a smart cookie." Mick Remarked.

"You asked for the best and the Chambers obviously thought she could do the job. They wouldn't risk their reputation, it means business and business means money."

"Well if she gets the LGA to meet costs will that include yorn?"

"For the appeal part Mick, we would still have the matter of the criminal damages case and I understand you want us to write your will."

"Yes, but that will be a simple job, Anything I have left, after this lot has been settled, I want to go to Frighall allotments society to subsidise any future rents. It's given me a lot of pleasure over the years and I want to make sure they can afford to continue."

Chapter 26

Gardening Leave

For some reason he began waking much earlier than he'd done for a long time. For years he usually went to bed around 10pm and woke at 6am without any alarm clock or any prompt from Josie…"Pit bus'll be ere soon." But, just lately he was wide awake at 4am and sometimes earlier.

He had had no trouble sleeping since he walked out of court and he knew the whisky had probably become his anaesthetic. Some evenings he started drinking once he had cleaned away his evening meal and some mornings he couldn't remember going upstairs, undressing and folding away his clothes but he was always awake early.

He decided that he may as well go to the allotment as soon as it got light. He had a lot of work to do now that winter was setting in. Beds needed turning over ready for the frost. He didn't use the protective sheeting that other tenants favoured. "Just protects slugs and mice" and there was a lot of horse muck to be fetch from riding school that abutted the allotments. It had to be collected, spread and dug in.

As he walked down the barrow path, Bill rushed passed him once again on his way to the final shift he would work at the colliery. "Morning Bill" but as usual there was no reply and he wondered if he too was destined to come to the allotment once he had passed away. As he neared his plot he could see two people working on the part he had given up. "The newbies are up early." He thought. "Must be coming before their work... Bloody hell no!" He could clearly see it was Mushy and Spud. "I need to see a priest or summat." He about turned and went home to do his ironing.

If the early mornings weren't working he thought perhaps he should try a late shift. At least after four thirty in the afternoon the only people down there were the plot holders who had hens to clean, feed and babies to steal… OK gather eggs.

For several days he grafted until well past twilight and then went home and surprisingly after a wash, and a meal he went to bed sober. OK he had a couple but at least he knew he was going to bed!

Brenda cornered him in the local supermarket. "Michael are you avoiding me? You don't seem to be coming down the garden much but every time I go down you've done some work!"

"No love I ain't. Oive decided that gooin to the 'Lockie' in the late afternoon is occupying me mind and keeping me away from the drink that yow and everyone else keeps warning me about."

"So why have you got a large bottle in your basket?"

"Reserves love, reserves."

"Michael, you should come down earlier there's a lot of folk who'd like to see you, and we need a committee meeting for you to update us and for us to tell you the progress we are making."

"There's a lot of folk Oiv bin seeing too, but OK, oyl come tomorrow morning and yes we need a committee meeting, we ain't had one since before Sid med a fool of is sen".. 'Med a fool of is sen' that's bloody Yorkshire tekin over." He thought. "Yes we need a general meeting as there is a lot I need to tell everyone, I'll ask Colleen and Bryanne to set one up for next week. And then after we will go for that meal." He smiled. "Accompanied by everyone else." He thought.

Back home his phone rang. "If that's a bloody call centre... "

"Mr. O'Rearden it's John Harrison, Can you kindly pop in to see us tomorrow about 2pm, Miss Morgan your barrister will be calling in. She has a meeting Dolethorpe Council's legal department and would like to update you on matters, while you are here we can finalise your will."

As promised he went to the allotments the next morning. As he walked down the barrow path he chatted with one or two, introduced himself to some of the newer tenants and waved to the plot holders that had long since become part of the compost up at the church yard and then he kicked his shed door, more out of habit than the need to scare the mice.

As he opened the door he was met by the images of Mushy and Spud sat beside the cold stove warming their hands on a fire that only they could see.

"I dun't need yow pair of fuckers today, piss off will ya and gie me some toime on me own."

They disappeared, so he messed about killing time until he was due to go to the solicitors.

Brenda nor any of the committee turned up that morning. "Typical, no wonder old Mushy gie up on is committee."

Washed, shaved, kitted and booted, he arrived at Harrisons five minute before parade.

"Please come in Michael" invited Harrison junior. "We have a few minutes before we expect Miss Morgan so maybe we can deal with our contract 'to wit' our charges for representation at Dolethorpe magistrates, and your wishes that we should be executors of your will there is also the matter of our safeguard that if…."

"Look if this is about money."

"No, No, we have decided to give you our services freely. All we ask is that we are mentioned in any press statements you give. We have asked Jamie Upton from the Yorkshire Clarion to join us later, as this will appear in the local news.

Shown straight in, she moved to the desk normally held by one of the Harrisons.

"Mr. O'Rearden" and then a pause followed by a smile.

"Fuck, its bad news" he thought.

"You'll be pleased to hear that there has been some major progress since we last met."

"I have just left Dolethorpe legal department after putting them in the picture. When my chambers submitted our plea for consideration by the High Court into your request for a judicial review… The LGA withdrew their support from Dolethorpe Council."

"You may be pleased to know your adversary 'Russel' has be put on, ironically, 'Gardening Leave' while a disciplinary investigation is carried out."

"Dolethorpe Council have decided, in their wisdom, that they have incorrectly asked you for a rent increase more than they are legally obliged to do. It would appear that the allotment officer is not an 'Executive Officer' and as such had no authority to ask for any increases without the sanction of his superiors in the 'Gardens and Recreation Department' who, in turn were obliged to ask the full authority, for permission to amended their earlier instructions that reduced allotment increases in line with inflation because of injustices that occurred in previous years."

"It would appear that your Mr. Russel was acting alone and with intent. Hopefully the investigations will support my view that he has acted above his position and has brought disgrace to the good name of the authority."

"However, in the matter of your appeal, Dolethorpe Council have acted without any powers to obtain rent increases from you and that is why the defence from the LGA has folded… You are not alone."

"When the National Coal Board ceased to exist they transferred all lands to County and District councils whilst retaining mineral rights and leeway's on and across all transferred properties, those rights are still held by the residual body set up by the Government to manage pensions and assets."

"For fucks sake… Come up for air." Mick thought when looked at her, his mouth must have been open, but she was steaming ahead.

"You will be aware that the 'National Coal Board' was privatised after it ceased trading. In doing in so it omitted to tell your society, and a lot of others too, that your, and their contracts, were being passed to the local authority, and therein lies the cruck of the matter."

"When the National Coal Board ceased trading in December 1984. They passed all allotment lands to County and District Authorities in clear contravention of 'Paragraph 9 sub-paragraph (1) of Schedule 29 to the Local Government Act 1972' which clearly states… 'If there is a Town or Parish Council in a particular area, then the responsibility for allotments within the boundaries of that town or parish lies with them. The District Council, in this case, has no powers to act in any manner over allotments."

"The result being that, where Local Authorities have sold allotment sites they did so without any cognisance that the National Coal Board, through their residual body, still held mineral rights to transferred lands and could, if they wished, move back onto newly built housing estates to reclaim those rights."

"Additionally, the Local Authorities in selling of allotments sites failed to tell the land purchasers who may sue. They are also required to pay plot tenants compensation when sites were sold."

"Your allotment society, and associations across the UK, were transferred incorrectly to County and District authorities who, have by law, no powers to raise rents or impose regulations upon or against you."

"Holy Fuck…" Thought Mick.

"The LGA have conceded the fact and I suspect that the RAAG will jump on board just for the kudos and will be broadcasting it in their magazines for some time to come.

"You will be aware that I have been to Dolethorpe Council's legal department and they have today accepted that four sites will be transferred to Parish Councils immediately. Your site will be transferred to Frighall Parish Council."

"Finally," she said with a wry smile, "On a good note… The LGA have accepted all costs and charges Mr O'Rearden." With that she said her goodbyes and left.

"Well bugger me… we've won!" exclaimed Mick "We've won!"

"There's more to come." Said a jubilant Harrison. "Jamie Upton from the Yorkshire Clarion is reception, He's hoping for a photo and he says he may have some news for you, he's been waiting on editorial approval for tomorrows headline."

"Can we have a picture outside these offices and maybe on your allotment?" Upton asked when they met him."

"Our free advert Mick."

"Good job oive got me suit on, what's tomorrow's story about"

"You Mick, your fight with Dolethorpe Council has caused them and a lot of other authorities to admit they have made errors when selling allotment land and when setting allotment rents.

"The bigger story will be that we are exposing Russel, Detective Sergeant Hurst, Patrick Salmons the managing director from Arsto Homes and Sid Davis your old adversary. They have been in league together in the hope of buying allotment land on the cheap then maximising their profits by selling executive housing."

"You were right the damage and the highest rents only happened on the most desirable building lands and not just around here. Davis was suckered into the scheme run by Russel and Salmons once he made it known he had a grudge to settle with you from the strike days."

"Patrick Salmons used them both and has history of buying up allotment sites. You were meant to be the fall guy and Hurst was supposed to have you painted as the villain so nobody believed you anymore."

"Hurst and Russel are on 'Gardening Leave' while investigations are being carried out. I suspect Detective Sergeant Hurst will take early retirement and leave on a pension. Salmons will probably be investigated by the National Fraud Squad. Russel may lose his job and if so will never work in for Local Authorities again because a lot of heads will roll over the sale of allotments."

"Once our story hits tomorrow, you'll be famous, the national media will be all over this."

"Your office sign will get a better advert than Tesco, no wonder yow've waived fees, crafty buggers, ar come on let's get me picture took before I start charging. Will oy get fan mail?"

"You may get your own TV gardening show." Harrison joked.

When they arrived at the allotment gates Mick and Upton were met by Windy Millar.

"Ey up lads, you're coming down a bit late. Have you come to take over Sid's plot?"

"Sid Davis's plot… As e jacked in?"

"You've not heard Mick… he's done a quick council house swap on the quiet with someone in Bristol who wants to be up here to be near their family, he moves on Saturday so his plot has become vacant."

"More good news." Mick laughed.

"Why what's happened?" queried Windy.

"Yow can read all about it tomorrow, By the way councillor… yow could be the new allotment officer!"

As they got to his garden, Upton asked him to remove his jacket and tie and to roll up his shirt sleeves and asked if had an old pair of boots or wellingtons in his shed.

Unexpectedly the shed was empty of any past friends. "Wonder where that pair of buggers are?" He thought.

He posed with a fork on one of his beds and Upton snapped him a couple of times, thanked him and left. By the time Upton checked his photo's he would see two extra gardeners stood behind Mick with their thumbs up and silly grins.

Left to his own resources he decided to continue turning the soil until twilight. It was becoming too much, his chest was hurting and he was breathing heavier and felt a little light headed. He decided it was getting too dark and that it was time to call it a day.

As he turned from closing his shed door he saw a young girl at the top of his path.

"Hey wot yow doing here, yow shouldn't be down here, off ya go home its gerrin dark."

"It's alright look, moms over there by the gate, she said you're to come now."

"Rose… Josie… Josie, is that yow?"

He felt a small hand grasp his.

Then darkness.

The End

Thank you for reading my book. It has been a long time in the making, and along time hidden from family and friends. Rightly so you may think!

My thanks go to the many characters I have met while keeping an allotment plot, the laughs and tips we shared have been priceless. Finally if the names of the characters are vaguely similar it's just a co-incidence.
Mick Reilly.

Copyright

Printed in Great Britain
by Amazon